~ 1 ~

Hobo Jake

The Ghost of the NEW Zoo

Hobo Jake
The Ghost of the NEW Zoo

ISBN-10: 1942731000
ISBN-13: 978-1-942731-00-9

Published by M&B Global Solutions Inc.
United States of America (USA)

Hobo Jake

The Ghost of the NEW Zoo

Jim Turner

Hobo Jake

Dedication

To "The Redhead," my wife Ginny.

She has tolerated me and my obsessions for over forty-five years.
That can't have been easy.

Contents

Introduction

This following is an interesting ghost story based in Northeastern Wisconsin, written for your enjoyment. Ghost stories are a mainstay of nighttime campfire conversations with friends and family. Many stories teach a lesson or relate a message; others are designed to scare the reader; and some are just for pure entertainment. Most require no technological enhancement. They are only limited to mental stimulation of the reader.

As my friend Louie would say, to understand and appreciate a ghost, you need to be aware of his flesh-and-blood human existence. This book presents the life story of Jacob Francis White, "Hobo Jake," as personally told to Louie by Jake's ghost.

Stories have been used since the beginning of time to aid in the learning process. I have a hard time identifying just how different it was in the past compared to today's standards. I write this for my own self-help based on research I have done on history in the Green Bay, Wisconsin, area. I use a fictional format to help tie the pieces together into a flow which makes sense. I hope you find this an entertaining and enjoyable read.

This is a story I heard years ago on a fishing trip with a couple of friends. As background, we were sitting around a campfire after a hard day of fishing. We were all tired and enjoying a post-dinner cocktail, and the conversation had come to how beautiful the night was and how wonderful it was to be spending it outdoors. We had finished our bragging on the day's success when one of the guys started to tell a related ghost story.

My intent is to retell that story, to entertain and inform as I had been. I know I learned a lot from the tale, and it helped open doors for future educational pursuits. In the process, I had a fun little experience. I hope to do at least half as good a job relating the story to you.

This story is based on one of the ghosts that haunt the Northeastern Wisconsin Zoo (commonly known as the NEW Zoo), located just northwest of Green Bay, Wisconsin. Jacob Francis White, nicknamed Jake, today acts as a guardian of the zoo and is part of a celebration each year at the Zoo Boo event in October. It carries a conservation message, and his story is a mini-snapshot of the history of Wisconsin.

Like many other flesh-and-blood individuals whose life stories have been passed down orally over the years, the tale I'm about to relay is best considered a legend. Billy the Kid, Buffalo Bill Cody, Paul Revere, Johnny Appleseed, Paul Bunyan, even George Washington's legends have been altered, manipulated, inflated and exaggerated in an attempt to mold into symbolic representations of a time or place, even expressing a point of view or philosophy. Jake's story fits in with these historic characters. Like theirs, historic facts are present, but what is fact and what is a bunch of lies is at best difficult to separate.

As such, I will take liberties to make the story flow as it was related to me. I shall also begin the story with the classic line "Once upon a time," as many of these legends should start with such an expression. Along the way, I will also toss in commonly held facts or beliefs by certain groups of people to support and reinforce some of the story specifics.

It was my friend, Lewis Black (we called him "Louie"), who first passed along this story around that fateful campfire. He was of French lineage and moved to Northeastern Wisconsin as a teenager from Chicago. He hopped around various jobs, finally getting hired and working at one of the paper mills in Green Bay until retirement. Late in life, he bought a house and lived in Suamico, just north of Green Bay along the west shore of the bay. He has since passed away and is buried in the Flintville Catholic Church cemetery, only a couple of miles away from the NEW Zoo.

Louie's move from Chicago was a result of previous gang membership. These activities had a major effect on his schooling, causing Louie to fall behind classmates and eventually drop out of school entirely as soon as he was old enough. He came to Wisconsin to live with his grandparents, as the job opportunities were greater in Green Bay.

One of his first jobs in Green Bay was as a towel delivery driver, with many of the Willow Street whorehouses on his route.

Willow Street today is known as University Avenue. Louie married and had four daughters. He loved hunting, fishing and the Green Bay Packers, but hated the cold weather. And he was not very tolerant of divergent points of view, especially when it concerned the Packers. He also enjoyed a frequent glass of brandy. And of course, he loved telling and retelling a good story.

Louie was superstitious, and in his opinion, an expert on many topics. Ghosts were one such topic in which he was a self-proclaimed expert. He further claimed to have developed a theory which was, in his mind, indisputable fact.

Louie claimed ghosts exist everywhere around the world, in every race and every religion. Ancient people and many people today, when asked if they believe in ghosts, would say yes. Louie saw himself as a quasi-historian and would reason that that many people can't be wrong. He would get a twinkle in his eyes and go on to explain, "In fact, one of the many ghosts in our area is located at NEW Zoo and named Jake. I saw Jake once, a couple of years ago. We had a little talk that night. As a result, he is the one I have the most information about. If you want to know about a particular ghost, you have to know their life story. If you don't believe me, you can check it out for yourself."

Louie's theory states ghosts haunt two types of locations: a place of tragedy, like a crime scene, suicide or fatal accident; or a place of strong emotional attachment, such as a cemetery, a childhood home, or a place full of fond memories. He would use his fingers to point or count as emphasis while detailing his theory.

He would go on to say ghosts are here only in a transitional state between "here and there," pointing toward the sky. "Most of them don't know they are dead." Once they accept the fact they are indeed dead, they are ready to complete their journey, and the number of individual sightings/hauntings decreases.

Finally, Louie would state there are four commonly occurring reasons for these sightings: The ghost either has unfinished business, an attachment to a location, a message to deliver, or is looking to exact revenge. This is the worst kind of ghost you can encounter.

I don't know how original Louie's theory was, but we would all nod our heads in agreement so he would continue with his story. Protesting or questioning his expertise would only bring out his verbal wrath.

Hobo Jake

Chapter 1

Jake's Early Days

Our story begins once upon a time in a faraway place. Actually, it begins with the birth of a male child to a single teenage female in Northeastern Illinois or Northwestern Indiana, in a shanty town on Lake Michigan near present-day Gary, Indiana. The child was the product of a rape committed by three drunken sailors fresh off a cargo ship in port for liberty. The year was near the beginning of the nineteenth century.

The rape had gone unreported and the female was blamed for being in the wrong place at the wrong time. She was further accused that she should have known better and was probably looking for trouble (you know, the whole "boys will be boys" reasoning). She did not survive childbirth, dying in the same bed, in the same room, in the back of the same shanty she herself had been born.

This young woman's father wanted to disown her and would have thrown her and her child into the streets to fend for themselves. Her mother was so in shock at the death of her only daughter that grief consumed her every waking moment. She saw the child as a physical link to her daughter and argued to maintain that link.

The child's grandfather reluctantly decided against turning the child over to a local church-sponsored orphanage, allowing his wife to take the newborn home. He reasoned the daughter's death opened a seat at the family table, and the new mouth to feed would be less demanding on their limited funds, because a child does not eat as much as an adult.

The grandfather also believed that if he did not allow the child to come home, his wife, in her grieving condition, would not fulfill her responsibilities and slack off on household tasks. He stipulated the birth not be officially registered, as "no child of Satan's spawn," would carry his family surname.

It then became Grandma's commitment to take full care of the child and not cause her husband any inconvenience. She unofficially named the child Jacob Francis White, but only referred to him as Jacob Francis in public and in the presence of Grandpa.

Jacob Francis started life unwanted, deprived of love and nurture. His basic needs were met, but the only warmth he received was when Grandma was alone with him. Even then, she could only act in ways her husband deemed fit. There was no supporting family to model later in life, and definitely no male role models to emulate.

At this time, the United States was going through a period of massive change, change like it had never experienced before in its short existence. There were forty-four states in the Union. Grover Cleveland was president. Most of the old French, British and Spanish territories had been included in these states' borders, while the presence of Native Americans had been reduced or neutralized either through defeat in battle or treaty.

There were about one million immigrants arriving on the coasts per year, seeking cheap land for farming and the abundant natural resources the country had to offer. Europe had deforested its continent, wood was hard to obtain, and the depleted soil from generations of overharvest and poor farming techniques caused a massive negative impact on crop yields. Droughts, disease and connected events such as the potato blight had reduced the quality of life on the European continent to the point where immigration was the only option. Most were not pursuing grand fortune, merely a better life for their family. And though the Civil War had been over for nearly thirty years, old resentment lingered. Reconstruction plans for the South had all but failed. Poor blacks continued to migrate north in search of jobs.

The first transcontinental railroad had been completed and many small, independent railroads were in operation between most of the inhabited towns, including those in the frontier and territories. Of note was the fact the width between the tracks was standard across most of the country, an efficient system allowing cars to be switched from one set of tracks to another without offloading the cargo.

Passage over bridges and through tunnels also became less problematic. Their measurement was equal to the distance between wheels on a wagon used on dirt roads of the time, which also happened to be the same as the distance between shoulders of a team of oxen or horses pulling the vehicle. Such measurements had been determined as early as ancient Rome, and continue as a very productive standard used even today.

The steam engine had been invented, revolutionizing transportation and creating the possibility for steam locomotives to pull trains by converting steam energy to rotational mechanical motion. The first steam-powered passenger carriage was used on the wagon roads of the United States. A Methodist Episcopal Church minister in Racine, Wisconsin, drove it as early as 1875.

Steam energy also was beginning to be used on ships, replacing sail power. It also was used in construction and farming equipment. Once engines became capable of producing ten thousand horsepower, they became the key component in sparking the industrial revolution in the United States. The country had previously been in the grips of a depression, and many small, independents farms were being foreclosed, their tenants moving to more populated areas in search of jobs in these new factory startups. The White family had migrated to Gary under such conditions, leaving behind a poor dirt farm for the lure of high-paying jobs in this new steel industry along the Great Lakes.

U.S. Steel had just opened a new plant in Gary, and Grandpa White had landed a job. The work was hard and heavy, with long hours and marginally safe working conditions in extremely hot environments. The pay was low. U.S. Steel would become the first billion-dollar corporation in the Americas a year into the new century.

Competition for these jobs was tough, as the unskilled-labor pool was huge and rapidly growing, a combination of immigrants coming to the New World and freed slaves who continued to migrate north, abandoning the economic conditions on southern farms. Farms, in general, were doing poorly, as competition for land was extensive and prices of land were escalating. Transporting goods to markets was difficult and usually required going through a railhead and/or a shipping port.

Gary, once a mere frontier rest stop, was now a booming community, a growing company town with churches, saloons, a school, a doctor, a thriving merchant district and greater safety – if only because of the number of residences. It was a step up from a slum and had some advantages lacking from the farm. There were even social events put on in town. Residents could buy goods in stores and access immediate services through purchase or barter. Almost every male worked in the steel mill. Those who did not were immigrants with trades or skills from the Old World, affording them a livable income in the small community. U.S. Steel had chosen this location because of the port and rail already located in the area.

Since before the region's old fur trading period, Native Americans used many locations along the waterways and lakes to establish trade or religious centers. They had created footpaths to and from these locations, following along the waterways and over game paths. Game had used these natural corridors, in part, due to their easy access to water. Water is a requirement for life, as are air and food.

Twenty miles away was the major port of Chicago, approximately a two-day walk. It was "the big city" because it sat at the mouth of the strategic Illinois River – yet another water highway into the interior. It had also been the site of an Indian trading center, with the French building Fort Dearborn there to protect and control the intersection. The French had done this at several other locations on the Great Lakes due to the fur trade business: Fort Winnebago, Fort Howard, Fort Mackinaw, and Fort Atkinson, just to name but a few.

Communities of settlers grew up around several of these locations. As westward expansion advanced, these locations flourished and even more settlers took up residence, due in part to the protection of the military garrison stationed at the fort. The British took over these forts after winning the French and Indian War. Many of these forts had been abandoned after the American War of Independence.

Military roads had been pushed through the woods connecting the forts. This helped in resupplying the forts as well as increased the speed in moving personnel from one to another. These roads at first were nothing more than dirt wagon routes, usually rutted and impassible at different times of the year based on weather conditions.

Small communities and stagecoach stops popped up along these roads, as they were heavily used in the move west by settlers and travelers. Traveling merchandise peddlers also used these roads to extend commerce to settlers in the interior and even to the Native

Americans that remained. The stagecoach rest stops were used to change teams, water and rest the horses, and usually featured a hotel were the weary traveler could spend the night, get a hot meal and maybe a drink. They were located nearly every ten miles apart, or about a day's walk.

These stops also provided security from the small bands of raiding Natives or outlaws who ambushed and robbed single travelers. The number of people at these locations enhanced the level of security. Rural churches also became a common feature in these small, growing communities. There had been legislation considered to require at least one church for every so many residents, similar to legislation established decades earlier in some New England states. And as New England had legislated early on in the Colonial days, if a town had a church, it had to have a tavern for social and political events, the function of which centered on a place to meet and vote. The roads were also used for the transportation of mail.

After getting settled in Gary, Grandma thought it would be a good thing for young Jacob to attend public school. If he were to make something of his life, she thought it crucial that he have the ability to read and write. Grandpa consented, allowing him to attend school as long as it didn't cost him anything. In his opinion, the kid didn't do a lick of work anyway and surely didn't earn his keep. And, of course, it would keep Grandma from causing him personal grief.

Grandpa continued to work in the steel mill. On paydays, he would usually get home late and drunk, spending half of his wages along the way. The result was the family was barely scratching by. Grandma turned to taking in laundry for extra income, helping to feed the family and maybe provide some little luxuries.

There were labor problems and threats of strikes against the rich companies. Efforts to unionize were meet by company resistance, with a few bloodied noses and blackened eyes, plus even a mysterious death or two. But Grandpa was able to continue working without many problems. He had his ideas and opinions on the matter and spoke only of them at home, at night, in a loud and extremely angry voice anytime he was drunk. Grandpa had even taken up the stinky habit of smoking tobacco cigarettes.

Jacob Francis attended school for six years officially and was in the fourth grade when he decided he had had enough of this school nonsense. He could make it on his own. It was then that Jacob ran away, heading toward the big city of Chicago. He told none of his friends he was going, as he feared they would rat him out to his grandparents, and Grandpa would thrash his hinder. Grandpa had never actually hit him, but had threatened to in the past. He would say, "Listen and learn boy, or I'll thrash your hinder so bad you won't be able to sit down for a week."

Jacob didn't want to hurt Grandma and hated to see her cry, so he just up and left. He figured he could read some and sign his name, count to a hundred if that was ever necessary, and he could make change, even though he had never seen much money in his life.

More important, he had street smarts. He and his friends had not wasted all their time on days they cut school. They had become skilled at stealing eggs and chickens from henhouses. They had learned the signs to watch for. A goose or goose droppings in the chicken area was one of these signs, as geese usually fill a role as security for the coop. A goose, when disturbed, sounds a loud noise that can almost wake up the dead.

The boys also knew how to steal apples out of backyard trees, sweet corn, tomatoes and potatoes out of gardens. Everyone had a garden and a hen house in those small communities. Some people even raised rabbits to add variety to the meat they ate. Rabbit was as tasty as a chicken, and tame rabbits couldn't run as fast as wild ones. Jacob saw an added bonus, as rabbits make less noise then chickens. Some backyards even had barns where the family cow was housed.

Jake's additional skills included knowing how to start a fire to keep warm. Scrap wood for fuel was all over the place. Coal cars on the tracks, waiting to be hitched to steam engines, were prime target. Sometimes passing cars would lose coal on a curve, a rough section of track, or when humped and jarred in the switching and hitching processes. Some firemen also would throw small lumps of coal at kids along the tracks as the train passed. Jake had made himself the target on more than one occasion so he could take a lump or two back to their secret hideout or even home to Grandma.

Jacob had a trusty pocketknife that Grandma had given him for his tenth birthday a year or so earlier. He was strong for his size and could run as fast as lightening. He could throw a rock a country mile, and he had learned a thing or two about bartering and horse-trading for the things he wanted. He was set to go. If there was something he needed to learn, he would learn it as he went. He was prepared for this life, and his mind, he thought he would never be more ready.

Chapter 2

~ 25 ~

The Challenges of Independence

The first place Jacob wanted to check out was the port of Chicago. Grandma warned him never to visit the port in Gary, as Grandpa would have his hide if he did. But now he was on his own and could do as he pleased. Grandpa would have no say in this matter, and anyway, he had learned in school this is a free country and we can do as we please, when we please. He had rights. Chicago was the big city and opportunity waited.

It took two days to walk to Chicago. The route was unmarked, and Jacob Francis was unfamiliar with the environment once he got out of his immediate neighborhood. He knew no landmarks, so just kept going. He did ask a kid along the way how to get to Chicago, but the kid just pointed and said, "I think it is that way." Luckily, there weren't a lot of routes to follow, so Jacob chose the one that appeared the most traveled. It was in use by the many vehicles involved in commerce and business.

Jacob Francis spent his first night cold and hungry after not finding any spoils to pilfer. He slept in a broken shipping crate he found in a vacant field in an industrial-looking area. It was a miserable night's sleep. He had never experienced such a night in his life and found himself, for the first time, afraid and lonely.

The new sounds of the night conjured up images of wild animals and demons in his young mind. For years, adults had used these imaginary creatures as a warning to young children at night. The intent was to frighten the child into good, soundless behavior so all could sleep in the house. People lived in much closer environments, and it was not at all uncommon for several individuals to share a room. These creatures lurked under beds and inside of walls, and only the dark would bring them out. Some might even eat misbehaving, noisy young children if they were found. His grandpa used such tactics. Jacob didn't want to believe in their existence, but had nightmares on occasion, with the creatures as the star of the mind's image performance.

Some people thought scaring a child with these creatures was a way to protect them. If the child strayed into anyplace dark, they could be injured or killed. If they traveled to unknown locations without permission, they might fall off the edge of the earth or into a big hole. It was a controlling method that played on the child's gullible mind.

Even children's stories designed to teach good behavior used ghosts, demons and creatures. The church was as guilty with its teachings of the devil and angels. Many parents had experienced these same teachings as children and unthinkingly passed on the stories to their own offspring.

Morning could not come soon enough for Jake. His sleep had been extremely light, awaking at every new and different sound. At first light, he found himself thirsty and hungry. He would have to attend to these needs soon, hoping they would not delay his travel too much.

Jacob Francis did not know at the time the human body can survive only seconds without oxygen, about three days without water and only about three weeks without food. Without any one of these essential ingredients, the body completely shuts down and death occurs. He was learning facts he had never bothered with in school, and he was learning them the hard way. The lesson of that night was a lesson he would not soon forget.

Upon breaking camp in the morning, Jacob Francis resumed his journey. That day, he planned to head in the direction traffic appeared to be flowing. He would go in the direction of the smoke, steam engine sounds and increased industrial and animal smells. He would be looking for places where horses were or had been recently, because where there are horses, there should be water. The horses were important in the transporting of cargo to and from industrial areas. Teamsters took care of their horses because a sick horse cannot work, resulting in teamsters not making any money.

Finding train tracks along the way would also lead to industrial areas, with most residences in close proximity to where they worked. He had witnessed this first hand at the steel mills in

Gary. One would think the port, the slaughterhouses, and the meat-packing plants would be similar. If he could find where workers lived, he would find their backyard gardens.

Overhead wires would also prove to be a landmark in his observations for the day. The plants and businesses were the first to get electricity. Residences were the last priority, and the wealthy were the first of that group. Jacob's plan was now a jumble of observations, including road surface changes, smoke on the horizon, overhead wires, horse droppings, and increased smells and sounds. He would figure out the rest once he got some food and water in his system.

Before leaving his current location, he decided to give it one last, quick look for puddles of condensation. The morning air felt moist and cool. Perhaps enough water had come out of the air overnight, and the dew could provide a sip or two.

This is exactly what Jacob found, and he eagerly lapped up the precious commodity. It was not enough to satisfy his thirst, but enough to give him encouragement to continue. He reasoned he had a sound plan to work from for the day. Now all he had to do was execute that plan. He was feeling confident, enthusiastic to forget the hunger pains for at least the present time.

Late in his second day of travel, Jacob Francis found a horse tank of water. He drank his fill without disturbing the horses sharing the tank with him. He also found a residential area and a candidate for filling his food demands. While watching a chicken coop and trying to figure out his plan of attack, the coop's owner came out of the house and made his way to the outhouse. This was the opportunity Jacob Francis wanted, so he made his move.

With his mission accomplished and without a peep from the hen, Jacob went bolting down the alley, chicken tucked under his shirt, when a voice rang out behind him. A hand grabbed his shoulder.

"Where you going, boy? What's you going to do with that chicken?"

He had not been restrained, but he froze in place anyway. He felt the blood rush to his head and felt another new feeling he had not experienced in the past: panic.

Turning around, he did not see the owner of the chicken like he feared, but a kid about his own age and size. The kid was smiling and said, "Why did you stop? I didn't stop you. Either you must not be from around here, or you're dumb or new to rustling up grub."

The owner was totally unaware of the thief and still enjoying his visit to his outhouse.

Jacob Francis replied, "What's it to you? I am going to eat it."

"This is my neighborhood and I call the shots around here, that's what," the kid said.

"So?"

"So? Don't be a wise guy. I could beat you up and take away your chicken. Or, as I was impressed by your style, I could maybe find you a job. But first, you would have to share that chicken with me."

"Okay. It is more than I can eat alone, and I do need a job. What's the deal?"

So started Jacob Francis's first business dealing outside of Gary. He and his new acquaintance shared the chicken that night and exchanged life stories. It was the beginning of a friendship lasting at least as long as it would take Jacob to become accustomed to this new environment of Chicago.

The boy's name was Ned, and he had lived in Chicago all his life. He worked a corner in a business area as a night newspaper boy. He bought his papers from the guy who owned the corner newsstand and sold them for what he could get after the stand closed and the owner went home. Some nights, it was a lot of papers. Some nights, fewer. It all depended on the foot traffic on the corner during the day. The money was good enough to live comfortably, given the situation.

Ned would buy the papers from the news stand at a discount just prior to the stand closing and the owner going home to his family. This was around 6 p.m. Ned would then sell what papers he could, proceeding to the saloons and red-light district near the docks and meat-packing businesses. His business would usually sell out before 11 p.m., but sometimes it would take until well after midnight.

Ned also knew where Jacob could find a free meal of thrown-out fruit or bread that was still good. He lived in an abandon warehouse and there was plenty of room if Jacob wanted to move in.

The rent was free. One only needed to be ready to move out at a moment's notice before the cops came to roust out the squatters.

As it turned out, the newsstand guy was looking for a couple more kids to help. His aim was to expand his business, giving some kids work during the daytime on other corners that did not already have a stand. Ned could move up to daytime and get a one-time reward, or bounty, for finding a guy for the night shift and the leftover papers.

Ned also didn't like the name Jacob Francis, as it was too formal. So he dubbed Jacob Francis just plain Jake. Jake looked more like a Jake, anyway, was Ned's thinking. It was a name Jacob Francis readily adopted. It stuck to him for many years.

They struck an agreement and sealed it in the traditional way of each boy spitting into his right hand and shaking on it. Then it was off to work for the first night. Visiting the rent-free quarters could wait until later.

The new friends chatted on their way downtown to the newsstand. As they approached a cemetery where a funeral had been held that day, Ned told Jake to hold his breath and follow him. Ned took off running. Jake did as directed and followed Ned. When they had passed the cemetery, Ned stopped and faced Jake.

"Wow! That was close."

"What was close?" responded Jake, looking confused,

"Don't you know anything?" Ned replied. "A funeral was held there today and if we hadn't held our breath, we could have inhaled the soul of the dead old fool."

"What?"

"Never you mind. I guess I got a lot of learnin' to do to you."

"What?"

"If you inhale a dead guy's soul, you get whatever kilt him and you'll suffer, dimwit."

"Oh, thanks, I guess."

They continued their trip to work.

Ned was proud as a peacock that evening, showing off his new associate. He introduced Jake to some of his regular customers and pointed out places to never go or risk losing your money and/or your life. Jake was an eager understudy and tried hard to impress Ned with his own bartering and business skills. They also deliberately did not sell the last paper; the cost to come out of Jake's cut of the evening profits. Jake would have something to cover up with when he slept at their new home.

Jake was particularly interested in the working girls they met either in the street or in the houses near the saloons. He had never seen such beautiful women in his whole life. He found it of interest that Ned referred to them as "hoes" when they weren't around, but "lady this" and "lady that" or "miss this," "miss that" in their presence. Ned told him they didn't like being called "hoes" and wanted to be shown some respect. He further explained this was the small price to pay for such good customers. At times, the hoes would even give out candy treats to a good newsboy.

"You don't pee or poop where you eat, so you don't bad mouth the ladies," Ned declared.

Jake was making good at the trade and established some of his own regular customers, ones he could count on for a sale every evening. Stealing chickens, eggs and garden vegetables became less important in his life, as he now could buy things on his own. Yet stealing still helped fill in the slow days' profits. The newspaper covers used for bedding were soon replaced with old grain sacks he discovered down on the wharfs.

Jake even found female friendship in an older lady named Madame Daisy, who ran a string of younger "ladies" out of a house on his nightly route. She could not have kids of her own and thought Jake resembled her younger brother. She had raised him after her own brother's death and still grieved his passing. She took to mothering Jake, and bestowed sweet candy treats quite often on him. On slow evenings or between clients, she would allow Jake to come into the kitchen, helping him learn to read the newspapers he was selling.

Jake wondered why this paper with all the words on it sold so good to the businessmen. She explained how the words told stories of wonderful people and places outside of Chicago. There were even funny cartoons that told stories or expressed different points of view. Jake took to reading and did it every chance he could. He also liked spending the time in the kitchen with this real woman and friend. He knew he would never see his grandma again, and this woman, with her soft hands and voice, reminded him of her. He longed to be held in Grandma's arms and kissed on the face.

When Jake did well with his reading, Madame Daisy would give him a big hug and kiss his forehead. He liked when this happened. He liked it a lot.

On one evening after he had done particularly well with his reading, Miss Daisy gave him his first paper novel. Jake had seen these before, but never bothered to investigate what they were. He was so proud of his new novel he could not wait to show it to Ned and read some of the story to him. This was his best possession ever.

Over time, he read the novel over and over, cover to cover. He also started watching for novels in the litter on the streets and became nearly obsessed with finding and reading during his free time. Some novels he even obtained by using his skill at stealing. Old habits are hard to undo. Of course, this reading time came when he was not playing dice or cards with the boys for money.

Jake also found some of the boys would pay him to read to them. They would pay mostly with cigarettes or beer found in bottles thrown out by the saloons or dropped by the drunks.

In his reading of novels and newspapers, Jake became familiar with two modern-day action heroes. These two men were the best examples of what men were all about to him, and they quickly became his role models. They were strong, bold, and skilled at what they did for a living. Jake wanted to be just like them and read everything he could find about these two individuals.

Chapter 3

Learning the Ropes From Captain Dan

For those in the know in 1907, Jack Boyd was the best river man in the north woods of Wisconsin and Michigan, and the subject of many pulp-fiction novels.

A French Canadian, Jack applied his skills at logging and riding logs down the spring flows on the rivers to the saw mills of these two states. The mild-mannered man barely spoke above a whisper. He was a master of three key logging positions, skills developed by the time he left home at the age of eighteen to pursue his interests. As a log scaler, he would mark trees suitable for cutting; as a feller, he would drop the trees; and as a bucker, he would trim the branches of the fallen trees and cut them into 16-foot lengths for transport.

He acquired skills as a teamster by driving oxen or horses that pulled the logs to the stacking areas along a waterway, placing them there to await the spring thaw and river flow. When the water conditions were favorable for the drive, the river men took over pushing the logs into the river and then riding them downstream to the saw mills. The drive was the most dangerous part of the operation, and few were completed without a least one man dying in the process.

Jack had acquired all the skills and was chosen by the company he worked for to be the on-river boss for most of his career drives. He was the best log walker and log birler, usually taking the most dangerous, difficult tasks himself. River men typically earned more than the common logger, so the job attracted the meanest, heaviest-drinking, fiercest-fighting and loudest-talking men of a logging camp. Many river men were French Canadian in heritage.

Jack was a small-framed, blue-eyed, pipe-smoking man among real men. Other teamsters knew him as a gentle handler of the animals, and they claimed he did more work than the animals he tended. He never used the whip or raised his voice when driving his team. He worked the woods during the winter and the drive in the spring. After being paid at the completion of the drive, he would spend about half his pay on drink and then return to his farm in Michigan for crop planting. He stayed with his family until after the fall harvest. According to company officials, Jack's family could have lived more comfortably if he had not spent so much of his money drinking on his way home or spent as many nights in jail for fighting during trips.

Many of the fights were the typical bar room brawls, but a few were because Jack's wife was a Native American and he took offense to being referred to as an "Injun lover." It was common practice, and encouraged by the church in Rome, to intermarry with the natives. These new wives, as well as any children born, could then be counted as converts for the church. The primary guise the French used to justify the expense of exploration of the new land in the days of Jean Nicolet and Samuel de Champlain was converting the souls of the native inhabitants to Christianity, and secondly to return to France whatever resources of value they found. As a royal enterprise, the French served the King. The fur market, and later the lumber market, was controlled by the French.

English colonists, on the other hand, had come as individuals looking to cultivate and possess the land. That difference was a key factor in the French and Indian War with England and the original colonies. Indians were feared and not trusted by the English colonists, primarily over the tension between land ownership verses general land use by all. The thinking at the time was natives practiced scalping as a religious ritual. If a brave did not scalp his defeated foe after a battle, the foe would meet up with him in the "happy hunting grounds" and the battle would continue. But if scalped, the ghost of the foe would be destined to wonder endlessly and not be allowed entry to those grounds.

The practice of scalping actually was introduced to the native inhabitants by the new arrivals. Beheading had been practiced in Europe for centuries, and the practice crossed the ocean with the new arrivals. A fee or bounty was paid first by the French and later the British for the heads of any dead enemy of the payee. Any man, woman or child had a corresponding fee. With beheading, carrying the head to the payment location was a bigger job than just carrying a hunk of head with hair on it. This is why the practice changed from the entire head to just a hunk of it in the new lands.

Jack hated it that others considered him a second-class person. He bristled at commonly held misperceptions regarding his relationship with his native wife and the history of scalping. With whiskey fueling his internal fire, he would fight.

Fiction writers paid less attention to the loggers and river men than to the pioneers on the western frontier or the northern fur trappers. Of this, Jake was unaware. But it wouldn't have mattered to him, anyway. Jake was fascinated by the allure of these real men, the wildness of the north lumber forests and rivers, the danger of encountering wild animals. Jake had never even had a pet because of competition for the food supply. The only animals he had experienced were the slum rats that tasted good when he couldn't find chicken or fish to steal. He thought one day he would take the big adventure and visit the North.

According to the reports he read, the rivers were teaming with fish and waterfowl, the woods alive with deer and other fur-bearing mammals. He had tasted venison once on the docks, and preferred its taste compared to the rats he had become accustomed to eating. He had read the fishermen along the big lake could fish two hours and have enough for their family for the entire winter. This same man could go out the next day along the shores of Green Bay and shoot so many waterfowl he would run out of ammunition, go home, and return the same day only to repeat the process all over again. The way he understood it, a man almost had to *not* want to catch fish or shoot waterfowl to come home without several meals.

The second man Jake enjoyed reading tales about was the Great Lakes pirate Captain Dan Savey.

Captain Dan, as people referred to him, was wanted by the authorities for his illegal activities on Lake Michigan and Lake Huron. He and his crew were suspected of running prostitutes to the merchant ships as well as transporting poached deer and other types of contraband for the right price. His biggest offense was commandeering a fully loaded cargo ship out of a friendly port, the *Nellie Johnson*. Dan had changed the name of the ship to *The Wandering* and claimed it as his own. This was a capital offense, and if caught, subject to the death penalty.

Captain Dan was also suspected of "moon cussing." On moonless nights, his crew would change navigation-light positions, the results of which could be catastrophic. Cargo ships that used the lights for guidance in the dark would run aground in waters they assumed to be safe. The crew on the cargo ship would abandon the ship out of the fear of sinking, some even drowning in the attempted escape.

As soon as the crew was away or in the water, Captain Dan and his ship would show up, not to offer assistance, but to start a cargo transfer before the Coast Guard or other ships could respond. The law allowed a ship finding an abandon ship to claim it and its cargo, like the child's game "finders keepers, losers weepers." This was a questionable tactic at best, but legal, except for changing the navigation aids.

Steamships were just beginning to replace sailed vessels on the Great Lakes, and once the Coast Guard started making the technological transition, their ability to respond became faster. This new capability was making life tougher on Captain Dan and his crew of pirates.

When the cargo that Captain Dan and his crew pillaged was safely on board, they quickly made sail to a friendly port to sell their goods, hopefully well ahead of the Coast Guard. These ports were welcoming and did not question how items had been obtained. They also served as safe havens for the crew and ship. The money they spent was as important to the townsfolk as the cargo itself. In fact, Captain Dan was married and had a family in one of these port cities, where he lived comfortably during the winter months when the Great Lakes were too frozen for shipping.

One evening prior to Christmas, Jake took the opportunity to visit the port and see the Christmas tree ship, the *Rouse Simmons*, a three-masted schooner he had read about in the newspapers. The story had fascinated him so much he jumped at the opportunity to see it firsthand. Every year, the *Rouse Simmons* brought trees cut in Michigan's Upper Peninsula to Chicago for the holidays. It was always the last voyage of the season for the sailors and a time of excitement for the families of Chicago. In late November 1912, the ship would go missing in a violent storm with the loss of all hands off Two Rivers, Wisconsin.

The day of Jake's visit, the docks had taken on the festive appearance of the upcoming holiday. Families had come down to buy wreaths and trees for their home decoration. The captain would always present the mayor a large tree for the town meeting place. There were usually free hot drinks of cocoa for all the people present, and maybe a cookie. How could Jake pass up this opportunity? It was a long-standing event in Chicago, and the boy wanted to see it for himself.

It so happened Captain Dan and his crew were in port at the exact same time. The nameplate on *The Wandering* had been changed in his efforts to go undetected in the celebration. Jake was selling papers and made his usual pitch to Captain Dan, unaware of who his customer was. Dan was impressed with the spunk and perceived fearlessness of the young lad. Even so, he refused to buy the paper. Instead, he offered Jake a deal.

Dan's cabin boy had fallen overboard recently and drowned. If Jake appeared at the dock before they sailed at first light, Dan would take him aboard and train him in the ways of a seaman – starting, of course, as Dan's cabin boy. This excited Jake immediately, but he had to give the prospect some serious thought. It didn't take too long, however. Jake ran home to his warehouse to grab his possessions. He did not tell his friends where he was going or even stop to say goodbye. He ran back to the docks as fast as his legs would take him.

The next morning, he began his first ship ride as a member of Captain Dan's pirate crew. Captain Dan Savey was the father of three daughters, and he needed a son to carry on the business. Jake reminded Dan of himself. Both had run away from home at a young age and were making it in an unforgiving world. He reasoned this boy could learn and grow, one day becoming the captain of his own ship. He had high hopes for this young, energetic lad.

One of the ship's strict rules was every man had to pull his own weight, or they would not get fed or a share in the bounty earned. This applied to Jake as well. He had duties on deck under certain docking and loading procedures. During days at sea, he was to attend to some of Captain Dan's needs, and in his spare time, assist in the galley with the cooks. Jake had read in his beloved novels – and Captain Dan reinforced the thinking – that if you were in good standing with the cook, you would make it aboard ship. Even the captain followed this simple rule. Cooks were in charge of who got what to eat, and when. Typically, the captain got the best cuts of meat and the freshest of fruits and vegetables. Next on the list were the cooks, then officers, senior crew, and finally deck hands. If Jake had a good relationship with the cook, he would get the same food as the captain and cooks.

The cook had the responsibility of obtaining the food ashore and preparing it underway. They had long hours aboard, but stood no duty watches – a blessing, as that meant they could stay in the warm galley and out of the bitter weather the ship encountered. It does get cold on the big lakes.

If one would treat the cook with decency and respect, they might get a special favor or a meal choice when the menu was drafted. Most cooks preferred the nickname of Cookie, and it was a source of pride to be recognized by that name. Jake had read of the same mannerisms in books discussing the Cookies of the logging camps.

Cooks also had the reputation of being the worst violators of the ship's rules. They were also some of the hardest people for the captain to discipline. Many cooks brought forbidden drink aboard or pilfered from the ship's supplies. Most captains were aware of this, yet allowed the cooks to take advantage of their position as long as it didn't get out of control.

Good cooks were hard to find and keep. Many captains made them part of the permanent crew, staying on board during winter's dry dock period. They did provide a level of security, but that was not the primary reason. Many cooks took advantage of this winter assignments as well. Some brought their girlfriends or wives aboard, living with them through the winter.

If Jake learned nothing else while he was aboard the ship, he learned the cook was the most important man behind the captain. Jake learned to work the sails and handle the lines as part of his deck training, and had a seaman-apprentice designation. The captain always found other things for Jake to do below decks in dangerous situations or when the weather was extremely rough above decks. Surprisingly, the crew seemed not to hold resentment for this favorable treatment as they respected Captain Dan, trusted him with their lives, and understood his plans for the young man's future. The captain had always been fair – at times even generous – with the distribution of bounty. That was what they were there for anyway: profit. The raping, boozing and other lawless activities were all but a bonus in their minds. It was just a way of letting off the frustration of being cooped up on the long voyages on the lakes. It was almost sport for them.

Jake had the opportunity to go on liberty in a friendly port with the crew. On one particular visit to a port, Captain Dan advised Jake in strong terms that he not fall into the trap so many sailors did. He said, "Don't mark yourself as a sailor. It makes it difficult to fit into or hideout in plain sight in civilian society." Jake had considered getting a tattoo, but heeded the warning, as the captain always knew best and he himself did not sport a single tattoo.

The first commercial steam ship on the Great Lakes was the *Walk on Water,* back in 1818. The increased speed and all-weather capability began a major shift in ship design for the lakes. The Coast Guard was only recently becoming better equipped. The slow process of changing over to steam-driven cruisers for patrol and interdiction meant they were retiring their fleet under sail. They also had heavier guns as a benefit of the faster, more maneuverable ships.

As fugitives of the law, the chances of being tried and hung kept the crew on their toes, watching for the new dangers on the water. In the past, they had been able to outrun the Coast Guard or lose them at night in the fog or on dark nights. Things were changing, though. The possibility of getting caught had increased.

After a couple of close calls with the Coast Guard and escaping to a friendly port near Chicago, Captain Dan put Jake ashore and told him to vanish for his own safety. *The Wandering* had recently come under fire from the Coast Guard. It had sent a shot or two over her bow, and the ship's crew heard the demand to heave to and stand ready to be boarded. The demand was ignored, however, and the ship barely escaped capture. It seemed the law was focusing in on ol' Captain Dan and his crew.

Jake was not aware Captain Dan had seen three seagulls flying together directly over the ship. The captain had been above deck to take in the nice day and get a breath of fresh air, and viewed the birds' flight as an omen of death coming soon. It was a widespread belief among Great Lakes sailors that if two or more gulls flew directly overhead, the ship's death was near. Most seamen were superstitious and took these signs very seriously. Danger, a man could deal with; but death was a whole different story.

When Jake reported aboard, he was given a brand new hammock to sleep in at night. The captain was concerned because his previous cabin boy had drowned after being washed overboard. He would take no chances. He feared the ghost of the previous boy would come back and do harm to his new cabin boy as revenge. It was a tragic accident and drowning is a miserable way to die, so there would be no testing of luck where Jake was concerned. Captain Dan even did a personal ritual of burning the old hammock on the fantail of the ship before throwing the ashes overboard.

Captain Dan also had a protocol of never sailing near Mackinac Island at the northern tip of Lake Michigan except at midday. A couple of the crew members claimed to have had personal experiences with one of the many ghost ships that sail Lake Michigan and Lake Huron. *The Griffon* in 1678 was the first to go missing. And even as late as the *Western Reserve* in 1892 were ships still reportedly disappearing. No wreckage, crew or anything was ever found. The spooky part is there have been numerous sightings of these ships over the years. These usually occur on moonless nights, with the ghost ship coming silently out of the darkness and disappearing if approached, as silently as it appeared.

The scuttlebutt aboard *The Wandering* was Captain Dan also had a personal experience with one of these ghost ships, spurring on his strict protocol in the waters near the island and the straits. It was also a difficult area to maneuver due to currents and obstructions just below the water surface.

Jake had never learned to swim, so when the Coast Guard's shots crossed the bow, he was afraid of being sunk and drowning in the cold water of the big lake. He was thankful to get off the ship with his life at the next port of call. As luck would have it, Captain Dan was captured two months later and brought to Chicago to stand trial for his life.

Jake was able to find his way back to Chicago. Standing on the same streets he had left for his high adventure on the lake, all he had were the clothes on his back and a pocket full of nothing. He needed food and a place to stay again, and he needed it fast. As best as he could tell, the year was 1908. He wondered if he still had friends there and if they would accept him back after leaving so abruptly.

Chapter 4

Changes in the Big City

Jake began a search for Miss Daisy or Ned, or really any of the others he had met and befriended earlier. He thought he would start his search at the warehouse he had called home, and then check the old man who owned the corner and sold him and Ned papers. This seemed like a reasonable place to begin and was as good of a plan as any.

After arriving at the old warehouse, Jake surveyed up and down for signs of Ned. To his surprise, it looked as if the place had not been used for months. None of Ned's possessions were there; no signs of food scraps, not even chicken bones. Jake found this evidence disturbing, and it dampened his enthusiasm concerning a quick resolution to his current food and housing dilemma. Because of the lack of apparent use, he reasoned he could at least stay in the abandoned warehouse until finding a more suitable shelter. At best, the place did not look to have been disturbed by the cops in a search for squatters.

Next on the list was seeking out his former newsstand operation. Luckily, the old man was still working when Jake arrived, even though it was past the man's usual quitting time for the day. He looked as old and cranky as before, only his beard was bit grayer. When asked about Ned's whereabouts, the old man claimed ignorance, saying Ned just stopped coming around. He added the neighborhood had changed and there seemed to be a new crowd of kids in charge.

This didn't completely surprise Jake. He recalled reading in one of the newspapers he found during the last few months that there were over one thousand active street gangs in the city of Chicago. The article went on to say the gangs' activities had become more and more criminal, and appeared to be organizing similar to the union movements occurring in the labor forces in factories along the Great Lakes. Strength in numbers to better protect one another's backs seemed to be the driving force behind the movements, and was leading to consolidation of gangs. Some of the gangs had graduated into the big time and worked for the organized crime families that were getting stronger as well. It was all about turf and profit. Jake wondered what had happened to Ned in the midst of all this change.

Last on the list for the day was Miss Daisy. She had always been nice to Jake, and he hoped she would at least allow him to sleep in her kitchen as long as he promised to not bother her clients. That way, he would not have to return to the vacant warehouse and the uncertainties of its safety. She might also be good for a meal if he offered to work for it by doing any odd job she might have available. He was particularly interested to see if she had any knowledge of Ned's whereabouts.

Miss Daisy looked the same – maybe a little more tired, but happy to see Jake. She said she was so worried about him and prayed for his soul every night. Jake didn't really understand the concept of praying, but thanked her anyway. But she also had nothing to report about Ned's whereabouts. Although, she had seen him awhile back with a bunch of the tough guys who were involved with the criminal element, as she referred to them.

Jake's day was not a total loss. His hope was fulfilled when Miss Daisy offered to share a meal with him and a place to stay the night, given the old rules of not interfering with the clients. All in all, Jake decided his plan had been successful, even though he had not found his friend Ned.

One night led to two, and two to four. Missy Daisy seemed to have an endless list of odd jobs for him, but Jake suspected she just liked having him around. No matter to him, living at Miss Daisy's was easier then living in the old warehouse, and he did enjoy her company when she was not busy with customers.

In return for his room and board, his job was to keep the furnace in the basement stoked with coal or wood such that the parlor and upstairs bedrooms were warm enough for the activities happening there. His room was actually a spot on the floor in the kitchen near the wood-burning cook stove, and he had to hide his bedding and pillow every morning in an empty cabinet in the kitchen. His jobs also included emptying chamber pots in each of the bedrooms every morning and between customers.

There were four other ladies working in Miss Daisy's house, so Jake was kept busy on active nights. The girls paid Miss Daisy a percentage of what they earned each day. If they lived in the house, as two did, they had to pay an extra weekly fee for food provided to them from the kitchen. Customers that took part in the food paid cost plus a profit margin to Miss Daisy. Jake provided a little muscle collecting these fees from customers who were reluctant to pay.

The formal parlor in the house had been converted to a waiting lounge. Amenities to the rooms always meant an up-to-date newspaper, a small wet bar, fully stocked with local beer, homemade wine, the best bootleg liquor available in Chicago, a small bucket of ice and a pitcher of water. Sometimes, Miss Daisy would take a large jar of pickled eggs as partial payment for her services or a large bushel of pretzels. These would be given to the paying guests on busy nights when there might be a long wait for a girl. The normal charge included one complimentary drink at the bar before and after.

The other addition in the parlor had been the installation of a pool table. This was not used much, but a few bets and dollars were exchanged over a game played on it. One of the reading tables had also hosted a game or two of dice or cards. It helped keep the clients happy and less irate while waiting for the service they expected upstairs. Jake, again, played a security and housekeeping role in these activities.

There was also a part-time cook who would work mornings, preparing the food for the house staff during the day as well as anything extra that would be offered to the customers that evening.

This arrangement worked well for a number of months and Jake was enjoying his new life. He enjoyed the company of the girls that worked the house, but Daisy had one strict rule for them: Jake was hands-off. Their services while in this house were for sale to the customers only. Jake was out of bounds.

She also advised him that he was to leave the girls to the customers, period. If he didn't obey this rule, he would be asked to leave and never come back. Jake had taken favorably to the house and the rules were simple, so he obeyed.

One evening, a few months into the arrangement, three roughnecks visited the house. They drank their complimentary drinks, went upstairs with the girls, but upon returning from being serviced, refused to pay. When Jake stepped up to try and collect the money, the three beat him, leaving him on the floor bleeding from the nose and knuckles. After finishing up with him, they broke two of the wooden chairs in the waiting room. Jake's eyes were swollen shut and he hurt all over. Miss Daisy and the girls closed up early and took Jake upstairs to treat his injuries. As the house's activities were illegal, there was nobody to whom they could report the incident. The next day, he rested in a walk-in pantry off the kitchen, continuing to mend his injuries.

A few days later, the roughnecks returned. Only this time, they brought an additional individual. This new person just happened to be Jake's old friend Ned. Miss Daisy and Jake both recognized him and were dismayed by his reappearance under such an unthinkable situation. Ned appeared to be the leader of this group and their spokesperson. He asked to see Miss Daisy to discuss a business deal. Reluctantly, Miss Daisy consented to a talk with Ned, as there had not been one customer all night. They sat at one of the tables in the parlor for a few minutes. Miss Daisy's face got red as a beet in anger. She constantly shook her head in disbelief, finally rising and running to the kitchen crying "No, no, no!"

Ned took that as his cue to leave. But before doing so, he shouted after the fleeing Daisy he would give her time to think about the deal, returning in two days for her final answer.

Business was extremely slow the next two days, and true to his word, Ned reappeared shortly after opening that evening of the third day. Ned and Daisy met for about twenty minutes. When finished, he went to the bar, gulped down a straight shot of corn liquor, and departed. Daisy told the girls to close for the night and gather the staff for a meeting. She had an announcement that involved everyone and walked to bar to make a drink. This was a very unusual thing for her to do, as she had a glass of wine about once a month– and usually only on a Sunday afternoon.

The staff gathered, the doors closed, and the sign put out saying business was closed for the evening. Daisy brought out a plate of sandwiches and placed them on the bar. The staff thought this to also be an unusual thing for her to do, as no customers were in the house. Once all staff was present, she told them to help themselves to a sandwich and a drink and sit at the table with her. They did as she directed.

She began by saying, "I love each and every one of you and have enjoyed working with you these past many months and years. It is has become apparent to me that now is the time for me to make some changes, so I am giving up management of the house effective tomorrow. You should get your stuff together tonight and be prepared for new plans from the new management about noon tomorrow."

She went on to say the new management had big plans for the house. They had purposefully kept the business away the last few days as a sign of their desire for all to see how sincere they were to the new plan. Individual roles for each of her current employees were included, and would be related to them at tomorrow's noon meeting. They would have the choice of taking the offer or rejecting it. It was up to each of them individually. That was all the information she had.

Miss Daisy closed her speech by repeating that she loved and respected each of them, wished them well, and told them to enjoy their drink and sandwich. Tears were streaming down her face. She tried to keep her voice from cracking, but was unsuccessful. She stood to leave and asked Jake to accompany her to the kitchen.

The girls sat there in shock, looking at each other in disbelief, tears streaming down their faces as well. They appeared to want to ask questions, but respected Miss Daisy enough to not probe. Jake followed her to the kitchen. She hugged Jake while kissing his forehead, and again said she loved him. She said she felt she had failed him and was sorry for not protecting him better. She told him none of this was his fault and it was, really, for the best for everyone concerned. She also advised him to listen to what they would say and make his own decision.

In the same breath, Miss Daisy also warned if Jake was smart, he would not get involved with these hoodlums. She had heard that they were still harvesting ice further up on the lake near Green Bay, and if she were him, she would catch the first train and head north. These jobs were seasonal, but honest and at good pay. They were always looking for strong, dependable help up there. And when the ice season ends in the spring, the circus in Baraboo hires roustabouts every spring for their summer tour schedule.

Jake listened to her words seriously. Tonight would be his only opportunity to think about the situation. There would not be a lot of time in the morning to do so.

Chapter 5

Running With the Mob

In the early 1900s, the Progressive Era was actively underway throughout the United States. Chicago was far from exempt from the political and legal reforms it brought. The city had a worldwide reputation as extremely violent, owning the world record for highest murder rate. Some of this soaring violence was a result of immigrants trying to preserve and maintain masculine authority brought from the Old Country. Economic pressure and unfilled expectations caused ego problems. Women's suffrage was a hot item of discussion, with opponents breaking along gender lines.

Much of the murder rate was domestic in nature, spouse killing spouse. Organized crime accounted for another major portion, as gangs with members between the ages of eleven to forty participated in unlawful activities for profit on a citywide scale. The largest majority of the gang members were between the ages of fourteen and twenty. Detroit, St. Paul, Milwaukee and other Midwest cities also had these organized gangs.

Chicago was the second largest city in population in the United States, leading to its nickname, "Second City." It was the involvement of its politicians in national-reform discussions that led to its other nickname, "The Windy City."

Horse racing had been outlawed in most cities nationwide because of the gambling that happened at the tracks. Football played at the colleges was declared a dangerous sport participated in by ruffians. Craftsman unions competing for jobsite control led to fistfights, work stoppages and strikes. Police were becoming better trained and more equipped as laws became increasingly restrictive on people's activities.

On top of all this, the nature of transportation was changing. Henry Ford introduced the first mass-produced, gasoline-fueled, internal-combustion passenger automobile. Black gold – oil – had been discovered underground in Texas, and its refinement became the propellant of these vehicles. Because of the mass production, the cost of a new car was in the affordable range for many of the working class and above. Within ten years, there were over 80,000 cars in the United States.

Road surfaces started to see improvements so vehicles could travel in excess of the national speed limit, established at ten or fifteen miles per hour in populated areas and twenty miles per hour in unpopulated ones. The biggest problem, beside the road surface, was the spooking of animals that shared the roads with these new cars. These speeds helped minimized this concern.

The first transcontinental automobile traveled from San Francisco to New York in a mere fifty-two days. The car was a Packard.

Gravel, dirt and even old plank roads previously installed to prevent cargo from getting stuck in the mud were being converted to concrete. Sidewalks along storefronts, which had been improved to wooden boardwalks, were further upgraded to concrete. Spring's problematic mud was becoming less of an issue.

The Panama Canal was completed in 1914, creating a shorter sea route connecting the Atlantic and Pacific oceans. This was over a hundred years after the Portage Canal brought together the Fox and Wisconsin Rivers in Wisconsin. President Theodore Roosevelt opened the Panama Canal from the White House with the touch of an electric button. The button set off a charge in Panama that opened the last flow stoppage in the system.

About the time Ford's cars were rolling off the assembly line, the Wright brothers were performing their first manned flight in Kitty Hawk, North Carolina. Less than twenty years later, the first airmail service began connecting New York and Chicago on a daily basis. The route followed beacons on the ground positioned about ten miles apart, each with an emergency landing field located at the beacon's base.

Since the Great Chicago Fire in 1871 – coincidentally the same night as the fire around Peshtigo, Wisconsin, that burned much of Northeastern Wisconsin on both sides of the bay – Chicago had been rebuilding and expanding. Now, many years later, Frank Lloyd Wright was designing and building houses in the Chicago area.

In Washington, Congress was discussing changes to the Constitution. In 1913, the Sixteenth Amendment was approved, authorizing a national income tax. This was the same year the largest dam in the United States was built across the Mississippi River in Keokuk, Iowa. The purpose of the dam was to control flooding while keeping sufficient depth and flow on the Mississippi for cargo barges and sternwheeler passenger watercraft navigation.

President Wilson was campaigning to keep America out of the war in Europe – a war getting uglier and uglier by the day. As a neutral country, the United States initially supplied both sides in the conflict. Great Britain had blockaded many German ports, but cargo continued to flow to Germany. Germany, in response, ordered unrestricted submarine warfare, sinking cargo ships of neutral countries that were transporting war goods and supplies to Great Britain.

In 1913, an American cargo ship, the *William P. Frye*, was torpedoed and sunk in the northern Atlantic with its load of Wisconsin wheat. Two years later, a German U-boat torpedoed and sunk the British passenger ship *Lusitania* with the loss of 1,198 lives, including 128 Americans. Finally, in 1917, German torpedoes sunk the American passenger ship *Housatonic*, pushing the United States to the verge of entering the war, now known as World War I.

Jake was still a little too young to fight for his country and could not sign up for any branch of the armed forces. What had his country done for him anyway, he reasoned. He had already been shot at by the Coast Guard, and that scared him out of his shoes and pants.

Maybe Miss Daisy's options were the best he had. But still, he had not yet heard what Ned had to say. Jake decided to speak with Ned before taking any action on his own. Jake was glad he could read, as it gave him information he used in making his decision that evening – a decision he felt would affect the rest of his life.

The meeting was held in the poolroom parlor of Miss Daisy's house. The entire staff was present, including Jake, much to Miss Daisy's disappointment and contrary to her advice. She had told Jake she had to take the deal. She added the beating he had taken caused her much distress, as he could have been killed. She could never forgive herself if that had happened. It could also be very costly to her, since no one would buy a house where someone has died under violent circumstances. People have a fear of ghosts haunting such locations. She would probably have to sell her house if the deal didn't work out, and the possibility of that was high. She would need whatever money she could raise from the sale.

After making the assignments, Ned looked at Jake and told him to come outside. Jake did so reluctantly, not sure what awaited him. Once outside, Ned told Jake he had big plans for him. That he had gotten approval to take him under his wing and show him the ropes. Jake was on the inside track because of their past experiences together, and he would soon be rich.

It was a promise that Jake eagerly took. Ned was to be Jake's personal trainer in the business. He could even live at Ned's place until he found one of his own. The full extent of the gang's plans was soon revealed to him. First, the gangs in Chicago were to consolidate and control all organized robberies in the city, then extorting money out of business owners for protection from further burglaries and damages. Second, they would gain control over all gambling and illegal drugs in their designated area of responsibility. Third, they would control all prostitution in that area. Last, but not least, they would control all alcohol distribution.

Whatever means they had to use to accomplish these goals was authorized as long as it didn't cause a customer revolt or police intervention. The "means" could be anything from intimidation tactics to murder. It could not be traced back to the big guys in the organization or there would be trouble.

Once these steps were in place, the organization would look to expand the overall area of influence. They wanted a monopoly in the region and all the profits – and the profits were huge, as they could charge whatever they wanted due to lack of competition. That is exactly what the big businesses of the day utilized as common practice. The mob adopted the same strategy. Jake knew this was not a plan Ned had conceived on his own. Ned couldn't even read. There had to be some brainpower up the line.

Most of the activities involved illegal actions, and most were related to the vices of citizens. The money did, however, sound real good and the risks seemed low. A bunch of police, lawyers and judges in Chicago were taking part in the profits and looked the other way, many times in disregard and against their official duties. No one wanted to get the federal authorities involved; therefore, all operations were kept strictly within trusted members of gangs.

Examples of federal laws and statutes affecting the mob and increasing risk were seemingly infinite: Horse racing was banned in Chicago in 1904 due to gambling being ruled amoral; the 1910 Mann Act made it illegal to transport women across state lines for immoral purposes; the 1912 International Opium Convention committed countries to stopping the trade of opium, morphine and cocaine; the 1913 creation of federal income tax with the Sixteenth Amendment; the 1917 Selective Service Act requiring men age eighteen through forty-five to register for the draft; the Eighteenth Amendment prohibiting alcohol was in effect from 1920 to 1933; and the Nineteenth Amendment gave women the right to vote. These examples only scratch the surface.

Law enforcement also improved with the creation of armed federal investigators, charged to uphold the laws of the land. New equipment and procedures left some local authorities looking like clowns, or at least the ones not on the mob's payroll. It was these new law enforcement agents that dubbed the gangs "the mob." Members didn't take kindly to the title given to them by the press and the cops, so it was never used around other gang members.

There is a side story of a federal raid on a drinking establishment in Green Bay, Wisconsin, another town notorious for disregarding the Eighteenth Amendment. The raid was launched out of a federal office in Milwaukee. By the time the feds had driven to Green Bay, the targets of the raid had been notified and the establishments cleared of any and all illegal substances. Communications and transportation systems needed to improve for law enforcement to stay one step ahead.

In fact, the Green Bay establishments got word of the upcoming raid through word of mouth and speed afoot, and notified all the establishments in the near vicinity of the imposing raid. The feds were sourly disappointed by their unsuccessful attempt. This is just one example of the ordinary citizen's lack of support of the amendment in Wisconsin and parts of other states.

Jake took to the gang's activities like a duck to water. He started his new career as a numbers runner between pool halls. Most of these contained large back rooms and a telegraph line for instant results from major tracks back East. He also provided some muscle in the collection of promised money from losing customers. He did some lookout jobs, watching for the arrival of the law and sounding the alarm of their approach.

Over the course of a few months, Jake received more responsibility. He responded with good results and attention to detail. He was even learning to drive motorcars used by the gang. Ever since Henry Ford's 1908 Model T made its appearance on American roads, the gang made sure to buy the best new cars for the business. It gave them major advantages as they attempted to keep pace with the police, who were constantly upgrading equipment as well as methods.

Jake was moving up in the organization, and the money moved up with him. He had gone from a roll of pennies – about fifty cents worth in his fist to give more impact to his punches – to brass knuckles. Within a year, he outpaced even that, carrying a firearm he could conceal in his waistband with his shirt tails hanging out.

Jake remembered the beating he had taken at Miss Daisy's that evening back when he was a kid. He remembered the massive cleanup that had followed. One of the things he had found on the floor after the fight was a bunch of pennies, and he wondered who would be wasting that money simply by not picking it up. His new position with the mob gave him insight into why the punches that night hurt so badly. In previous fights, he had never sustained so much pain from a few well-placed strikes. With the mob, he was learning to take advantage of others. There are no rules in a fistfight; one fights to win.

Driving cars was the activity Jake enjoyed most. It gave him a new feeling of freedom, and he took every opportunity he could to do it. He was also learning about how to keep the car in service longer, spending free time hanging out in garages with mechanics. He would do odd jobs for them so they wouldn't request he leave the garage area.

Jake remembered the long walks in his youth, the first from Gary, the second after being put ashore by Captain Dan. He could now cover the same distance in a fraction of the time. The legal speed limits were increasing as well, and the wind blowing by the open windows was refreshing. He liked the attention he got driving by the people he passed as they walked. There was even a horn he could use to honk at pretty girls. He really wanted to become a full-time driver, but in the gang, the rule was you take the assignments that come your way. You never question or complain, or you might not wake up the next day. So being a driver was not in the cards for Jake.

The passage of the Eighteenth Amendment opened the door to bigger profits in the running of illegal drink. Even in the days of Captain Dan, alcohol was smuggled into the Chicago and other cities by ships coming to port from Canada. Now, with a total prohibition of alcohol, keeping customers supplied took on a bigger part of the business plan. With no legal access and a distribution system already in place with the Canadian product, expansion was easy. The demand did not drop and saloon owners were going to lengths to keep their businesses open and free from interruption. They were willing to pay top dollar for good stuff. The big drink producers were forced to close or convert to a different product lineup. This left a void the gangs were willing to fill as they grew their business.

Family farms in the wheat-growing areas had always produced drink, some for personal use, some supplied to local friends and family. Money was tough to earn on the farm, and by simply gearing up their production, they could make a significant impact on their profit. Gangs with distribution systems already in place were willing to bear the risk of transportation. Combined with improved road structures in the rural areas, they offered an ideal alliance for farmers willing to increase their production and fill the market. The few cases in which a farmer would refuse to cooperate sometimes resulted in their barns being burned or livestock disappearing.

Turf warfare between rival gangs was not uncommon. Running gunfights in the city streets, drive-by attacks from one gang on another, as well as gang executions of key rival members received a lot of press coverage. Add in the threat of the federal agents, and it made for exciting times to be in the gang. Jake was making more money than he ever thought possible. Jake was not around the gunfights, although he did learn to use some of the gang's weapons. He always carried a gun with him, though more for personal protection and intimidation rather than to kill.

By 1932, Jake had moved up in the organization and was given an assignment that made him very happy. Because of his driving ability, accuracy with a gun and his head for business, he was selected to drive north to Wisconsin with a couple of the gang leaders, their lady friends and a handful of bodyguards. Before leaving Chicago, he said he was going on a paid vacation and was excited.

Jake had a secondary assignment on this road trip. After delivering his passengers, he was to escort a couple of truckloads of moonshine to Chicago for quality testing, as the gang wanted to expand into this area and gain control of the production. He was then to return north and pick up his passengers, finally returning them back to Chicago.

Jake had never been this far north in Wisconsin and only knew his river man idol, Jack Boyd, had lived and loved this part of the country. The scenery was reported to be utterly beautiful, with miles of unspoiled timber, abundant with fish and game. He had never known the woods growing up in and around the big cities. The only woods he had seen were from the deck of Captain Dan's ship; but then he usually had a number of tasks to do and could not spend time looking around much.

Everything went as planned during the first part of the assignment, and Jake unsurprisingly fell in love with the north woods environment. When he arrived back in Chicago with the moonshine safe in his possession, his only hitch came in reporting rumors of rival gang activity in the part of Wisconsin he had just visited. Reports of activity from both Detroit and St. Paul gangs were suspected.

This news was not welcome and changed Jake's second assignment. Another car was sent to pick up the leaders, while Jake and two carloads of men were sent to confirm the rival's activities. He was advised not to engage them unless absolutely necessary. The extra guys were along primarily as insurance. With these new orders, Jake returned to the north woods to be gone no more than a month. Again, he was excited about a visit to this beautiful area. At the time, Chicago was controlled by two competing gangs, the North Side Gang and the South Side Gang. They did battle from time to time over turf – the infamous 1929 St. Valentine's Day Massacre was evidence of this – but tended to join forces against the competition from Milwaukee and Detroit. Often, it was difficult to determine which gang a job was meant to appease.

Jake, under Ned's tutorage, had joined the old Market Street Gang during the Circulation Wars between Chicago newspaper publishers. The Market Street Gang was one of many street gangs in Chicago in the early 1900s, eventually becoming the North Side Gang. Ned had been mentored by a man named Dean O'Banion at the onset of "The Noble Experiment," better known as Prohibition. Dean and his followers got started providing muscle during the Circulation Wars and progressed on to bootlegging. They had little involvement with prostitution or selling the girls from houses on turf they inherited to guys on the other side of town, as had been the case with Miss Daisy's girls.

Jake had heard the "Purple Gang" out of Detroit was making inroads with the St. Paul gang to cut Chicago and Milwaukee off from the high-grade moonshine produced in the Northeastern Wisconsin area. Their own product from Detroit was considered more rotgut, or bathtub gin, rumored to kill or maim the drinker by causing blindness.

Jake visited New London, Wisconsin, forty miles west of Green Bay and the center of the "Alky" ring's business. One of the biggest moonshine producers in the area, The Fern Dell "dairy farm," had a capacity of eight hundred gallons per day. Since the days of lumbering, many of the small farms in the area supplemented their income by producing and distributing home-grown products during the winter. Wooden shingles had been the mainstay for years and had made the port of Green Bay the biggest shingle shipping port in the world. As the land transitioned to wheat growing, many shingle operations had been converted to stills. These stills could be found all over the area, with wheat and pure water the primary raw materials.

Wisconsin had maintained its status as the number two wheat-producing state in the country, behind only its neighbor, Illinois. However, the over-harvesting of wheat was taking a serious toll on the soil. A transition was occurring, with wheat farms converting to dairy. It was easier work with a high-demand product. Most of the dairies maintained their stills, which had led to the "Alky" ring, establishing a reliable pickup and transportation system to get the product to market. The system was similar to the milk routes. Today, the stills are as well hidden as they were for Jake, sprinkled across every corner of Northeastern Wisconsin.

Jake was able to confirm the presence of the two rival gangs and their efforts to squeeze the Milwaukee and Chicago gangs out of the area. At a chance meeting one evening in the small crossroads village of Flintville (just northwest of the current NEW Zoo), the two gangs became entangled in a gun battle. This was much to Jake's disgust, as he had orders not to engage them for fear of an all-out war in Chicago. The battle raged for about thirty minutes, resulting in Jake himself being seriously wounded. Two of his men were killed and they had to make a hurried exit from the scene. Jake's men pulled him and his dead companions into the cars and drove off.

Because of the serious need for medical attention, they found a local veterinarian who treated in a barn on one of the moonshine farms. Jake gave the order that under the cover of darkness, the men were to slip into the small cemetery at the Catholic church at Flintville and bury the dead, undetected by the parish priest. The burial was more to hide evidence than for any religious reason. But for Jake, he gave some thought to the fact many of the gang leadership crossed themselves when they witnessed death. This gave him an indication they held some religious superstitions regarding ghost haunting the living.

Jake's injuries were no longer life threatening, but he was still weak and needed to get back to Chicago. Once the dead had been buried, the depleted gang turned tail and headed south as fast as they could. Years later, in the telling and retelling of the tale, it is said the group actually met the sheriff as he was responding to the veterinarian's telephone call reporting the gun battle and injuries. The version includes the men actually passing the sheriff's vehicle on the main road, totally without incident.

Jake's rising stardom in the organization was tarnished by this defeat. Not only did he return empty-handed and with no good news, he had also engaged the rival gangs, breaking the orders he had been given. He had lost men in the process. This had been a real opportunity for Jake to shine. As this was his first leadership test and he had failed, the assignments directed his way and corresponding pay fell. Only because of his past friendship with Ned and Ned's high recommendation was he spared the death sentence – a sentence typically demanded under such circumstances.

As no leader demanded the sentence and no other bad marks were on his record, Jake skated on mob punishment. The repeal of Prohibition in 1933 also had a negative impact on Jake's well-being. Jake realized just how bad a spot he was in and started the process of evaluating his future plans. As with anyone facing a major decision, Jake did an immediate review of his actions, what he had learned in the past, and what advice he had been given by trusted friends and family. The old "what do you know, what do you think and what have you been advised." He needed to make some choices about his future.

Miss Daisy had once told him stuff happens to good people totally outside of their control. You do the best you can based on the situation. Life isn't fair and sometimes you lose. She had also relayed the importance of learning from your mistakes and changing your behavior, or you are very likely to repeat those mistakes in the future. Jake reasoned all this out, thinking, "Ok, good, but so what?"

Miss Daisy had continued on to say a person did what they needed to do to get by. This made sense to Jake. It was part of the survival instinct. She had also said there were consequences for a person's actions, and to expect differently was foolish and self-destructive. Most rules had a reason for their establishment, and deciding which to follow and which to break was the challenge everyone faced in life.

Ned had said that work was for suckers. You have to take care of your needs, as nobody else cares or will do that for you. The most important thing in life was three square meals each day and a warm place to take a crap. This made sense to Jake as well. Ned further said if you don't take advantage of an opportunity quickly that is available in your favor, you are as stupid as the other individual that gave you that opportunity. You have to compromise, negotiate or lie that you would comply with the particulars set by the offer. In other words, take advantage of the other person's stupidly and weakness. It was all about getting ahead, a game of survival. Ned believed at the end of the day, the guy with the most money was the winner. Jake understood this from his playing of dice and cards. All is fair in life and war.

These were the only two people Jake had found of any value to him in his life since departing Gary. Daisy had once said that Jake was liked by everyone and had the ability to adapt and learn. This skill would be good for him in the future. Ned had said Jake was smart, had skills and potential, and these traits would benefit him. This had been the basis for Ned's recommendation to the gang leadership for admitting Jake into the business. Jake's current task was to sort through this information and make a decision quickly.

Chapter 6

Searching for the Show

Daisy had told Jake after the beating at her business that if she were a strong young man like him, and in his situation, she would not trust Ned and his new friends. She had suggested two other places for possible employment.

Maybe she was right, and her advice remained worthy of consideration. He still didn't like the cold, and ice harvesting was definitely a cold-weather activity. The circus, on the other hand, might satisfy his desire to see new places and meet new people. This also was a seasonal job, but the combination of the two had some serious potential in his current situation. He could disappear from the Chicago gangs. He might even make enough money with the circus that he would not have to do the ice-harvest work. The skills of handling canvas and driving the circus trucks seemed to fit with his previous jobs of sailing on the Great Lakes and driving for the gang. He already knew most the knots required for canvas handling.

It was then Jake decided to check in again with Miss Daisy. The next day he would go see her, as she was still in the house working as a manager. He had run into her a couple of times during his gang association, stopping by to check on her well-being. He had slipped her some money each visit as he was flush and she was still struggling. He didn't understand the warm feelings he had for her, especially when she would hug him and kiss his forehead. He had desired to help her at those times and did what he could with the cash in his wallet. Maybe it was because he felt he owed her for the time he spent living in her establishment. Maybe he also craved seeing her, as it had been quite some time. He missed her, the warm feelings he got in his loins. He would go visit the next day.

They sat at one of the new poker tables and had coffee and a shot of whiskey after the customary greeting hug and kiss. Miss Daisy seemed pleased to see Jake, and he felt ten feet tall at the way he was received. They talked about what had been going on in their lives and the outside world in general.

Daisy's girl business was gone, transferred to another gang's jurisdiction. But the saloon business was in good shape, growing even better with the repeal of Prohibition. She still did not prefer working for the gangs, but one had to do what one had to do. She thanked Jake for his past generosities and said they had been a major help in the current Depression, just keeping the wolf away from the door. Her cut of the profits was severely impacted by the gang's take, but she could make it with a little effort.

Jake opened up about the situation he found himself in as a result of his defeat in Flintville, talking at length about options for his future. To Jake's pride, she agreed with his thinking and suggested he execute his plan sooner verses later. She would miss him, but he could write and keep her up to speed on his activities if he wanted.

They talked briefly about Ned. He had been involved in the 1919 Black Sox gambling scandal. It seemed Ned had been among the gang members responsible for getting the Chicago White Sox players to throw the World Series by losing the eighth game of the best-of-nine series to the Cincinnati Reds. Through pitchers hitting batters, an error here and there, and a batter striking out at key times, the game and the series swung in favor of the Reds. Gamblers who had bet on the underdog Reds to win the series made big money due to the White Sox losing. Court records suggest the eight players involved in the fix were paid $70,000 to $100,000.

Rumors circulated into the 1920 season that the series had been fixed, and finally a grand jury was called to investigate. Star outfielder Shoeless Joe Jackson was one of the eight players charged and brought to trial, but no player or coach was found guilty due to insufficient evidence. However, baseball commissioner Judge Kenesaw Mountain Landis banned all of the players from the game for life.

Ned also avoided prison for his role, despite being instrumental in setting up the deal. He later found himself in trouble for other crimes and sent to federal prison, where he would die as a result of a riot in the cellblocks. Jake had heard some information concerning Ned when the incident happened, but had no knowledge of the grave aftermath.

Jake also admitted to Daisy he had no place to spend the night. The Great Depression had been rough on him and the work very slow since the Flintville incident. He had lost any money he had saved playing dice and cards, and was so far behind in his apartment rent that he had moved out two days earlier and now slept in his car. He guessed it only a matter of time before the gang's bill collectors would catch up to him and he feared spending another night in his car.

Daisy told him he could stay with her for two or three nights, but if he truly was on the blacklist of the gang controlling her establishment, for his safety – as well as hers – he would have to limit his stay. She requested he stay upstairs in her private apartment and not come downstairs, no matter the noise or disruption below. She would make sure he had food and drink, but even that was not an unlimited supply. The Depression had been personally tough on her as well, and money scarce.

Jake agreed to her conditions and promised he would only stay a day or two. He included that he would sell his car for a grubstake if he could find a quick buyer with cash. If not, he would dump his car someplace out of the way, someplace safe. If he could not accomplish that, he would push it into the river to keep the heat off Daisy and her establishment.

Four days later, Jake said his goodbyes to Daisy and walked off to the nearest railroad mainline. Little did he know that would be the last time he would see Daisy, as she would die of polio two summers later. Polio had claimed the lives of millions of Americans, and outbreaks took their toll every year as warm weather appeared. He made sure to get his goodbye hug and forehead kiss, and fill up his stomach before he left.

Jake walked briskly, feeling on top of the world with a good plan in his head. He even was whistling a little tune he heard on the radio. He had promised to keep in touch by mail, letting Daisy know where he was. Maybe he would come back and the pair of them would have a good reunion together in a season or two. They would go out for a big meal and do the town up right.

Rail transportation had improved and access to rail was easy. One of the politicians in Iowa even boasted to Congress in 1935 that there was no place in the state more than thirty-five miles from a rail line. During 1916, the federal government established a highway system for defense. Military supplies and equipment could use these roadways to quickly transport material from coast to coast. These roads were usually labeled by single-digit numbers, such as U.S. 6. The highway system was expanded in 1922, interlinking all states and major cities in the federal system. These newer roads were usually labeled by a two-digit number, such as U.S. 29. East-west highways used even numbers, while north-south highways used odd numbers. These were good pieces of information for a traveler to know, thought Jake.

Another piece of information Jake believed useful for a hungry traveler was how over seventy percent of households in the country were now supplied with electricity. Keeping an eye out for houses without lights turned on could mean a location of easy pickings for food or money, if one was interested in going that far. The biggest problem would be homes where occupants retired for bed early. Of course, one should listen for a radio playing in another part of the house, which would also provide a red flag. That would indicate a need to take that house off the potential target list.

Hitchhiking became popular in the United States during the Depression. Jake had never used this method for travel, but he thought it a good option. He would keep an eye on the driver for inappropriate behavior, of course. He could take care of himself, after all, but a free ride sure beat walking between rail stops or where the trains did not run. Jake was surprised how easy it was to get a free ride just by sticking out his thumb. He was further surprised by some of the questions he was asked by the drivers. The strangest was an inquiry if he was a ghost. The question came up even before the driver opened the car door to inquire where Jake was heading. When he answered no, the door swung open wide.

It was the spring of the year, and from what Jake knew, this was the time the circus would typically hire staff for the coming summer tour. Jake thought his timing was good. He felt sure he would easily secure some kind of a job. It had taken less than two days to get to Baraboo, Wisconsin. Now the plan was to find the circus' winter headquarters.

Jake stopped people on the street to ask directions. To his displeasure, a stranger told him, with a hardly disguised chuckle, that the circus had not wintered there since 1918. The Ringling brothers had bought out Barnum and Bailey in 1907, and the company moving its headquarters to Florida in 1919. None of the show's equipment, people or animals remained in Baraboo. The Ringling family still owned acreage outside of town, but it was all but vacant.

Jake was disappointed in the news. He figured he or Daisy should have known that information due to reading all their newspapers. He did know P.T. Barnum had been a publisher of the books on action heroes he had read back in his newsboy days. He did not know Barnum had died in 1891, and it was the family business that the Ringlings had bought from the Barnum heirs. How could he be so uninformed?

It was true he had not done much reading while employed by the gang. But how could Miss Daisy miss this key information? Would she still advise him to go north to join the circus if she knew it? He would have to do some major re-thinking about his existing plan, that was for sure.

Barnum had been a New York business man. He dabbled in a mixture real estate, stock trading and publishing, as well as owning the circus, but he did not perform or travel with it. The Depression had been tough on the circus industry, as people had little money to spend on entertainment. Many small circuses had gone broke while larger ones consolidated business into a few big operations, just as the Ringlings were doing. Meanwhile, the labor movement had unionized the performers, and that added cost to management, which further cut the bottom-line profit for many small, one-ring organizations.

The Ringling organization was a big, three-ring circus. From its headquarters now in Florida, they scheduled three, two-year routes across the United States. The routes were divided into three tours: a red one by train, a blue one by train, and a gold one by truck. Each route included a three-ring circus. The red and the blue routes went opposite directions, one west and the other east. They followed the major rail lines and did big-city sights. At one time, a single route could have five acres under canvas. But there was a movement to use existing expo halls and stadiums, reducing this need for canvas. The gold route was more for the rural performances, but still was a big-production show. Jake considered this new information and decided he had never been to Florida. What would he lose if he gave it a try? He would catch the first train heading south. He would follow the circus.

Jake made it to Florida by rail in a matter of two days. He was amazed that less than a week ago he had been in Chicago. The weather was much warmer here, almost like mid-summer back up north. The people he met had an accent he found amusing at times, and at others hard to understand. He even wondered if they were speaking the same language. His task remained bent on finding the circus.

Jake spent two days searching and searching. He asked strangers to please give him directions, but nobody seemed to have any idea what he was talking about. Getting hungry, Jake walked into a diner along one of the main streets in Sarasota and told the owner he would work for a meal. The owner asked where he was from and what he was doing in Sarasota. Jake explained he was an out of work performer in the circus and wanted to hook up with the circus that wintered here. He also said he was originally from a small town up north.

The owner asked if he was out of work because of the consolidation and so many small circus failures because of the economy. Jake answered he was. Jake thought there was no harm in telling a lie if it got him work. The owner said he also had been a circus worker and was displaced when the small, one-ring family operation he worked for had gone out of business a few years back. He said most of the other people he had worked with had gone into the carnival business as operators of amusement rides, sideshows, or food venders. A couple of families had banded together and ran some of the midway games of chance. He, however, decided to settle down in one location, opening up the diner. The traveling show was way too much time away from his family.

The diner owner also expressed the disgust he held for some circus people, as they seemed to hold the people who now worked for the carnivals as second-class or inferior. The disrespect was terrible.

Jake sat listening to the owner, still hoping for a meal, nodding his head in constant agreement. A little sympathy seemed what the owner was looking for, or at least that was Jake's take on the situation. He was learning a lot from this man, and Miss Daisy had always said a person learns something new every day. He was learning and gathering important information. After about forty-five minutes, the owner asked Jake if he was hungry, to which Jake heartily answered he was starved.

"Sweep the floor, take the garbage out back, and wash the dishes in the sink, and I'll fix you a steak and eggs," the owner said.

Jake did as directed and later enjoyed a great plate of food. Jake asked the owner if any of his friends in the carnival business still in town might need some help, as he was available and ready to travel. Jake knew it was the time of year the carnivals went north to county and state fairs, volunteer fundraising events, and other smaller venues and events compared to their main circus operations. He told the owner he could drive a truck, set canvas tents and was an all-around mechanic as well as a short-order cook. He stretched the truth a little, but it might help him in his quest of a job. Jake additionally told the owner his name was Kent Clark. He had read a superman novel while a newsboy and changed the hero's name. He didn't want to use his real name in order to protect himself from any connection to the Chicago gangs. The owner said his name was Phil, and they shook hands.

Phil remembered a couple of families still in the area, promising to talk with them later that evening. If nothing else, he might be able to find where the carnival they were going to meet would be located, and when. This was just in case Jake wanted to just show up at the job site and see if he could snag some work. At each location the carnival stopped, the organization usually hired a couple of local roustabouts for security and odd jobs. Jake thanked Phil and they again shook hands.

Phil had good news the next morning. One of his friends had hired driver who had not yet shown up. If he didn't show by noon, Jake had a job – at least to the first stop on the circuit. According to the friend, the driver was a stupid drunk and probably locked up in a jail someplace.

Phil went with Jake to meet his carnie friend, Fred. Phil introduced the two and told Fred that Kent (Jake) was an out-of-work circus person displaced by consolidation, just like they had been a few years past. Fred informed Jake that he had a job at least as far as the first stop. If his regular driver did not show before they moved onto the second location on the circuit, Jake would have a job for this year's circuit. The pay was poor, but the deal provided a place to sleep and would put food in the belly. Jake took about ten seconds to think before agreeing to the terms. This time, it was Fred and Jake shaking hands.

One thing still bothered Jake. It involved the bizarre question he had been asked about being a ghost back while hitchhiking. He asked his two new friends what that was all about. This led to a couple of stories – one from each – about ghosts traveling on the highways, usually at night.

Locals along one point in the circuit claimed a case where a young woman walking home from church one evening was hit and killed by a passing car. Since that day, on the anniversary of her death, she flags down a passing car and requests a ride to an address down the road. The address is the local cemetery.

The second story was about the driver Jake was replacing. It seemed two or three years before, he had been stranded on a rainy, dark night. He claimed a car approached him very slowly with no lights on. As the car provided temporary shelter from the storm raging around him, he quickly climbed into the backseat only to find no one at the steering wheel. The car continued moving at the slow and steady pace. As it approached "dead man's curve," out of nowhere a hand came in the driver's window and steered the wheel so the car could safely take the turn. Once through the curve, the hand disappeared. The curve had been the scene of many a car wrecks involving death on rainy nights such as the one he was experiencing. He even swore the story to be true on his mother's grave.

Jake found it interesting his two friends were laughing so hard while telling their tales that tears were welling in their eyes. Jake asked why the laughter, to which Phil replied, "The guy got beat senseless two days later." It seemed he was in a local bar down the road when two strangers walked in and took him outside and beat him. Upon entering the bar, the strangers had shouted, "Hey, that's the drunk that jumped into our car the other night in the rain when we were pushing it." The man got out of the car and ran across the field screaming once the car made it around "dead man's curve." They said he had taken a crap in the backseat where he was sitting when he saw the hand on the steering wheel.

Jake saw the humor in the situation and joined in the laughter. He remembered from his mob days in Chicago the thinking was that if you had two eyewitnesses to an event, they would have two different stories to tell and swear to the factual nature of their individual recounting. He had a couple of associates who had gotten off at trial due to the doubt it caused in the jury hearing their case.

Chapter 7

Carnies and a World War

The circuit usually ran from April to October, starting and ending in Sarasota. There was free time while at each destination, and Jake could find side jobs for cash. He could also help Fred around the food stand he operated, which translated into a pay raise. The extra money helped him purchase a few drinks at each stop or carnival food from the other stands at a discount. Jake felt he had landed on his feet and was hiding in plain sight, safe from gang justice. He also decided not to tell Miss Daisy, as that might cause her problems and it might jeopardize his new identity.

Things went smoothly. The driver never appeared, and by the fourth stop on the circuit, Jake was feeling like a full-blooded carnie, although the old-timers called him rookie. He fit in well with the carnival. The routine was fairly standard on a weekly basis, and all you had to do was follow the routines and rules. Travel was usually on Sunday and Monday. The setup of the midway, sideshows and game booths, and testing the rides usually happened on Tuesday. Wednesday was opening night and the show ran until Saturday night.

Closing was usually around midnight, with fireworks signaling the official finale.

Some sites had special events scheduled Thursday through Saturday nights. These events included everything from grandstand concerts and tractor pulls to stock car races. Fairs also usually included animal judging and cooking competitions, with an awards ceremony on Saturday. Teardown and site cleanup began as soon as the fireworks were over. Off-duty carnies and a few full-time management personnel bouncers provided some security for the set-up and parking area for the trucks, campers and some living tents.

A typical carnival included amusement rides, food, beer and merchandize vending, games of chance, thrill shows, animal acts, freak shows, and most had a burlesque review. These were located along a central midway. Customers paid an entrance fee at the gate that went to the management organization. Individual shows and the booths were mostly owner-operator run, so there was an additional charge for each of these. The owner-operators paid the management organization a fee covering the cost of facilities and electricity that the organization paid the site sponsor. Included in this list were most of the logistical necessities such as water, ice, vender delivery of supplies, shower and bathrooms, mail pick-up and delivery, and trash disposal, among several others. The rides were also owner-operator run, so additional charges were collected there as well.

The burlesques had special performances or add-on shows once inside their tents, for additional charges, of course. Services similar to those Miss Daisy and her girls provided in Chicago could be purchased. Police at the locations kept close eyes out for these activities and watched the beer tent closely. Police were paid by the sponsor location. Nobody got rich, but nobody starved. A good management company helped assure a good circuit season. If the location and sponsor organization was happy and the customers were happy, it was a good deal for guys like Jake.

Carnie people took care of carnie people, at times even tossing a cop who was trying to get freebees. Local police usually handled young punks, but the carnies kept a watchful eye for troublemakers and dealt with them swiftly, many times before the locals even got involved. Grandstand events were the sponsor's, as were the revenue from these events. The sponsor would schedule months, even years ahead, planning around events or holidays. The management organization kept his owner-operators informed to schedules and locations, plus any feedback from the sponsor locations. If there was trouble with the local police, individual operators were warned. In certain situations, they were even requested to leave the carnival by the management organization. Everyone has rules for operating.

Jake spent some of his spare time around the fortune teller and the magic shows. These sideshow booths fascinated him, and he wanted to understand – even learn – how to do some of the tricks. There was also a tent that never had anything scheduled in it. It was be used for limited storage, but mostly for card and dice games. Jake also spent some time here and made a few bucks. Many of the midway games were rigged to prevent customers from winning big.

The card games were no different, stacked against the visitors in favor of the house. Jake liked having an advantage at these games. The carnival workers didn't refer to the customers as "suckers" as Barnum reportedly had, calling them "marks" instead. It was an unstated expectation these activities be kept secure, and the carnies policed the action for the marks who tried to get payback.

Jake was also interested in the Ferris wheel and its operation. Since the wheel ride had been introduced at the Chicago World's Fair in 1893, it had become a standard carnival ride. Chicago had built a permanent amusement park featuring a midway Ferris wheel and roller coaster after the fair. Jake spent part of his spare time with the owner-operator, trying to learn as much as he could about the popular ride. It was a good spot to watch the pretty girls that always attended the fair. Different girls at every location, but still similar: eager, excited and giggly.

Traveling carnivals seemed nomadic by comparison to the workers in the Chicago amusement park. This was probably the source of a misconception in the eyes of the general public. Migrant workers and immigrants from southern and eastern Europe were more nomadic in their efforts to make a living. "Gypsies," as they came to be called, was the negative term generally applied to these more recent immigrants. Carnies routinely received the same label, a fact most did not appreciate. Many also found the term "carnie" offensive, which was similar to the warning Jake had received years before about calling Miss Daisy's girls "hoes." They preferred to be called amusement-park operators, seeing as the general public held a fairly low opinion of Gypsies.

The term "Gypsy" does not refer to any one nationality or religion. The most recent immigrants were from disparate locations economically and politically, and their customs and traditions were different. The stereotype had grown from some of these differences. They were nomadic in general, moving as family units that enjoyed the outdoors and were good at living off the land. The extended family was important in their culture. Their music and musical instruments were also very different, sounding Far Eastern and labeled exotic. Music and dance were immensely popular, and many famous entertainers, both on stage and in the circuses, came from their clans. They married early into pre-arranged marriages. The women were flashy in their youth, wearing bright colors, and bangles and gold bracelets. Some of the trashier women had gone into burlesque. This, in turn, led to another label of promiscuous.

In Europe, Gypsies were predominantly known as horse traders, leading to a claim they were swindlers and thieves. Worst of all, some individuals, in an attempt to earn a few dollars, read peoples palms and/or told fortunes. Of these, some even claimed to be able to talk to the dead loved ones of a mark who had a few cents to waste. One of the girls Jake took a fancy to practiced communicating with the departed. She revealed to him the dead talk to us every day, we merely need to listen and learn. It was her job to help facilitate that. Jake thought he had heard something like this before. He couldn't quite decide if it was from Miss Daisy or possibly even his grandpa. Maybe both.

Some of the traveling carnival families had a history with these immigrants and used that knowledge to run sideshow booths that featured these skills. These booths always drew a crowd and marks' money. Gullible customers are easy to identify and fleece. Get a couple of beers in them and the organization hits the jackpot.

Most Gypsies, migrant workers, carnies and even hoes were just a bunch of hard-working individuals trying to make a decent living. Jake quickly sympathized with them. Wasn't he, himself, doing the exact same thing?

Jake spent a lot of time around the carnival sideshows, feeling some of those feelings for the young Gypsy girls he had felt for Miss Daisy years before. He resisted the urge to take any action, though, as he wanted to do a good job and be welcomed back the next year. He talked some of this with his boss, Fred, and received guidance. Jake thought he should also talk to Phil on the subject when they got back to Sarasota, given he was invited back for the next year's circuit.

Not much went on in the traveling carnival that was not soon known by the whole ensemble. It was hard to have secrets, but it was a great place to hide out from the world. Jake did complete the circuit without major incident. Not only did he get a bonus at the end of the season, Fred asked him to join him and his wife for the following year's circuit. In addition, Fred wanted Jake to stay the winter with them in Sarasota, helping to repair and upgrade his business. He said he could not pay Jake much, but he would talk to Phil about hiring him part-time at his diner once back in Sarasota. Things were looking good for Jake in his life as Kent Clark.

The new arrangement worked. Jake enjoyed the life of a traveling amusement park operator. He kept himself out of trouble by remembering the warning Ned had given years before: "You don't eat where you poop."

Young Gypsy women came and went without Jake getting overly friendly or involved. Owner-operators left the show. New ones took their place. Attendance grew for a couple of years, but then started to decline as World War II loomed on the horizon, taking a dip into the entertainment business. Europe was in chaos, after all.

At this point, Phil was nearing retirement and Fred was thinking of it as well. Fred did not want to go out, however, without trying one more business expansion. He was considering getting rid of his straight truck for a bus with open sides and an awning. Instead of having to set up a booth at every location, he could just park, open the sides, and start selling. Everything would be moved in place. He thought he could pick up some equipment from owners leaving the business and expand his own in the old booth by adding cotton candy, peanuts and popcorn.

He wanted a partner and gave Jake an opportunity to buy in by investing some capital. Jake had no stash of cash. He spent his money almost as fast as he earned it. He had always been that way, and old habits are hard to change. Why save for a rainy day when today the sun is shining without a sign of a cloud in the sky?

The rain always ends up coming, though. As of December 7, 1941, the United States was involved in another overseas war. Gasoline and certain foods were being rationed for the war effort. Railroad and highways were being dedicated to movement of war supplies and equipment. The draft was implemented. Even lights were restricted at night so the enemy would not be able to detect targets on the ground as easily. Many of these changes had a big effect on the carnival, ultimately hitting the earnings of workers.

Jake had never signed up for the draft, nor had his alter ego, Kent. He felt he might be safe from a call-up. The problem was his job security was being threatened and he would have to find other employment soon. The fear of this ultimately drove him to decide to enlist, as it also happened to be the patriotic thing to do. It was world travel, a job with pay, three squares ones a day *and* a warm place to crap. It was Ned's advice plus some.

Fred would understand, as would Phil. The only problem was neither Jake nor Kent had a birth certificate and could not verify his age. In fact, he wondered if he was so old that he might be over the eligible age to enlist. But this problem could be easily solved. Jake knew a guy who knew a guy whose brother-in-law was into printing, and would print anything for the right price. In his favor, Jake heard the military was enlisting almost everybody who could breathe and walk upright. He might need another new name, though. An easy problem to fix, he would adopt a name he had read on a tombstone at a local cemetery – a guy who would be about the right age. Henry Black Jacobson fit the bill perfectly.

Before the spring roundup even occurred, there was almost a certainty this year's circuit would be canceled. Jake took this opportunity to sign up for the Army, listing truck mechanic and driver as his skills. Henry Black Jacobson enlisted in the Army and was assigned an occupational specialty of motor transport operator and mechanic. His birth certificate confirmed he was born in 1912, which made him thirty years old on his last birthday, Christmas Day, 1942. He went by the nickname of Hank. He obtained the new name and birthday from a tombstone of a child that had died at the age of three, so there would be a record on file if anyone wanted to check it out.

Jake reasoned the kid didn't really need his name anymore. Jake made it through boot camp without distinguishing himself either positively or negatively. He was on a world adventure soon after graduation, the first real graduation he ever had (although his records indicated he was a 1939 high school graduate). Shipboard life had not changed all that much, but the situation was much different. Jake had lots of time to play cards and barter for necessities with his fellow passengers. This was a new environment from his days as a pirate.

Once on land in Europe, Jake proceeded to demonstrate the skill and efficiency he had learned driving for the carnival as well as for the gangs in Chicago. After a short period of time, he was assigned to be the general's personal driver. This was one of the best driving assignments in the whole Army. You lived, ate and slept in the best available facilities. You got the same royal treatment as the general's staff and officers, which was far superior to the everyday grunt infantryman. You would go where the general went; you did what the general did. A good deal, Jake believed. And yes, there were three square meals a day, and they were always hot.

Jake was able to distinguish himself even in this elevated role, acquiring a combat decoration for his effort. After a visit to the front, Jake was driving the general back to the secure billet area when a German artillery shell exploded in the road behind them, killing the general instantly. The general's body flung forward and protected Jake from taking any major impact. Jake rushed the general's dead or dying body back to the rear area hospital. It was there the general was pronounced dead. All good things come with rank and privileges, and because he was the general, he received a purple heart and silver star for saving Jake's life, posthumously. Jake received a Purple Heart with a combat star. He also received a promotion and reassignment to a non-combat unit.

Jake continued in the non-combat role after the German surrender. The unit was doing clean-up operations across France. The girls were everywhere and happy to see the well-fed American G.I. when he came around. For a few cans of C-rations or a candy bar, the girls would service the liberators and supply them with good wine. Jake was in his heyday and used his bartering skills often.

One evening, Jake and a couple of his friends borrowed a jeep to go see some local "talent," as they referred to the girls. After partying well past the bed-check time at base, the boys decided to drive back, drunk on French wine. Speed was no object. They were already late, so they drove as fast as the jeep would go. Missing a curve in the dirt road, the jeep crashed into the only tree in a two- or three-mile circle. Two of passengers were killed outright while Jake, the driver, had a broken back and leg, plus a deep cut on his face that eventually would cost him his eye.

The jeep had a radio that the survivors used to call for help. It didn't arrive until nearly three hours later, transporting them to the field hospital. Jake had a choice coming out of this event: He could take a court marshal and get a dishonorable discharge, or he could lose his rank, his occupational specialty, and accept a transfer to the Pacific Theatre of Operation. With the second option, he could probably get a general discharge if he kept his hinder out of trouble. He took the deal, and after a short recovery time, prepared to ship out to the Pacific.

While en route to the Pacific, the war ended. Jake and his unit were scheduled to be part of the invasion of Japan in the hopes of ending the war. The atomic bombs changed all that. Once they arrived in the Philippines, they were transferred back to the States for discharge. As Jake had signed up in Florida, he would be discharged in Florida. That was the rule.

Jake actually found this to be to his advantage. He hadn't saved any money during the time he was serving his country. The best he could imagine he would get was a general discharge. No benefits went with a general. What he had in his pocket when he hit the States was his ambition to start his new life. If he wanted to buy into Fred's business, he needed to raise some quick cash. Jake figured he could earn a few bucks, maybe enough to get by gambling on the trip.

It took a number of days for the ocean transit, and then a few more to take a train back to Sarasota. That should be plenty of time to earn enough to buy into a carnival booth. He wanted to have at least as much as Fred had requested before he had enlisted. Of course, his name would need to be changed back to Kent in Sarasota.

The ship was filled to capacity with returning soldiers. Most of these guys had never played cards or dice in any serious manner in their past. They would be easy marks. Jake made about three-quarters of the money he thought he would need on the ocean transit. There would be fewer guys on the train, but again, these were the same type of happy, returning servicemen. Still easy to beat in a game of chance.

The train from California to Florida was a shorter trip. To Jake's disgust, his fortunes changed this time around. By the time he got back to the train depot in Sarasota, he had been wiped out. Again, he was alone, broke, and forced into finding a meal. The past few years had been nice in that his food and shelter needs were handled by the government. He had not been overly hungry in a long time and did not want to experience it again.

Jake thought he would check in with Phil and Fred upon his return to find out what was happening. Now it was even more important to re-establish old ties with friends and associates. On the train back to Florida, Jake ditched his uniform and returned to the name he had used in Florida, Kent Clark. He kept the Purple Heart medal. It had given him a second chance once before, getting a better discharge and avoiding the court martial. Perhaps it would prove helpful in the future.

However, there was no hiding his facial scars from the accident. Maybe they might help in some way, too, Jake optimistically thought. Only time would tell. A wounded veteran might get a break after he returned. The way it stood now, he had no veteran's benefits or even special treatment in jobs like the post office was offering.

Jake found out Fred had bought Phil's business from Phil's widow. Fred had then given up his carnival business completely, as profits were so down due to the war, rationing and extra factors Jake craved to know. Fred told Jake he might be able to help him out, but only for a few days at best.

Jake was on the streets with empty pockets again. Well, almost empty. He did have a Purple Heart, which might get him favorable consideration by a future employer. The sad truth was the award, in his estimation, would not even get him a cup of coffee in value, even hocked at the pawnshop. Additionally, he was getting older, and the people that had helped him in the past were far away, dead or both.

Chapter 8

The Making of Hobo Jake

Jake once again found himself alone, living on his wits. He would have to come up with something quickly, as Fred had said he could stay only few days and it had already been a week. Jake felt he had overstayed his welcome.

Times were tough, and there were droves of men just like him, home from the war and looking for meaningful jobs. Most of them had an advantage of honorable discharges compared to Jake having a mere general discharge. This was a huge red flag to the knowing employer. At least he had escaped a bad conduct or worse yet, a dishonorable discharge. Most of the potential employers he had spoken to were patriotic and proud of the victory the country had in the recent war. There was a lot of goodwill toward the returning servicemen. Offering a job was a way to say thank you to the returning heroes.

Maybe he had made a mistake throwing away his uniform, keeping only the boots and medal. Guys were scoring with the women and getting free drinks all over the place as a result of continually donning their military garb. He had only gotten a drink or two, or even consideration for a job, when he decided to pin on his Purple Heart before entering establishments.

In order to receive even more favorable treatment, he would change his nickname on occasion, saying things like, "My name is Hank" or "Kent," "but the guys all called me Ike." This depended on who he was talking with and where. Ike was the nickname of one of the famous war generals, Dwight David Eisenhower, who would later run on his name for the presidency and win. His campaign slogan would be "I like Ike!" Jake had met him once while driving for his general back in Germany. Jake liked him. He thought the train and special cars the train pulled exclusively for Ike and his staff in Europe was the classiest way to travel. That train, years later, would be displayed at the National Railroad Museum in Green Bay for public admiration.

But too many people in Sarasota already knew Jake as Kent. He had no other real choice but to move someplace else and start over. But where could he go? What would he do? He didn't even have a traveling stake or grubstake to cover his expenses. If he survived without them before, he figured he could do it all over again. Stealing had always been an option. Jake only had to deal with situations as they came up.

Jake had another major disadvantage, however: the ugly scar on his face. His youthful handsomeness was now gone. The scar was an attention grabber for sure, but in all the wrong ways, scaring more people than Jake liked to admit. He was getting older. In the Army, he had passed for his late forties, when in reality Jake was much closer to sixty. His appearance was beginning to catch up with the fact.

The scar and the Purple Heart enabled him to drink free on a number of occasions as long as he told a good story about how he had earned both. He had already invented a decent tale, and with each retelling it became grander, more detailed. One would almost think Jake had won the war singlehandedly. Sometimes, he would tell a story about being a steward in the special train, and that the train car was haunted. He invented storylines on how he had to deal with the ghost, and on some occasions claimed the ghost had injured his face.

Maybe the scar, the medal worn on his shirt and a good story to explain both would be an advantage in getting considered for a job. At least it probably could get him a meal or two on his upcoming trip. But a trip to where was the real question. He had yet to determine his destination.

Before enlisting in the Army, Jake had taken a fancy to a Gypsy girl at the carnival who talked to the dead and told fortunes in a booth. Maybe someone with the current carnival family, an old-timer, had some knowledge of her family's location. Gypsies were recent immigrants from Europe who did seasonal jobs or provided entertainment and traveled as family units. He saw himself as a good fit into their society.

The girl was a beauty and easy to talk to. He had experienced feelings toward her like he had felt toward Miss Daisy. He thought she had felt the same toward him. A few years back, they had taken a picnic basket one slow afternoon and ate sandwiches together under a tree by a lake at one of the circuit stops. He had been advised to not act on those feelings at the time. But now was different. Maybe one of the old-timers could steer him in the right direction. If not, maybe he could revisit some of the circuit stops they made that year and find her on his own.

The girl's family was homeless, like he and most everyone else. They were all looking for a home to apply some of their skills. The carnival had been their most natural option. Many had worked in European circuses, where the negative stereotypes as devil worshipers and witches made them alien to others, outcasts in nearly all societies.

Jake decided to use the name Ike and go on a quest in search of this lovely girl. He hoped he could make a life with her. He was getting older and was tired of traveling alone. The warm body of the girl in his bed at night would be a great improvement. He enjoyed the travel and would be willing to put down roots anywhere her family decided was right, just as long as he could be with her. He was willing to work hard and learn new skills, ones that were needed. His plan was taking shape. He remembered someone once saying, "Success comes before work only in the dictionary, not in life." Jake was not sure what that meant exactly, but so what? He had a plan to execute.

The old-time carnival owner-operators were of no help, so he started his quest by hoping on a freight train heading north. He would try to avoid the Chicago area, but he was interested in seeing what changes had occurred, remembering Wisconsin was still up there by the big lake. He had enjoyed his short stays there. There were many circuit stops in Wisconsin, Upper Michigan, Minnesota, Iowa and Illinois. He would check them all if necessary.

One of Jake's first observations was there were more guys traveling free by train. They were calling themselves "hobos." Jake figured this to be a shortened form of "homeward bound" or "homeless boy," but it didn't really matter. They all spoke of rules of being a hobo. They camped in groups in "hobo jungles" and used certain vocabulary words they all seemed to know the meaning behind. Jake reasoned this might make the journey easier seeing as the "bulls," or railroad security cops, had increased their efforts to limit the number of free riders. There might be better security in numbers.

He had read years before of the "Underground Railroad." Escaped slaves used this network of secret routes and safe houses during and after the Civil War to travel north. They had a way of communicating that minimized certain threats to their safety, and for finding food and lodging. It was a relatively safe passage route. Apparently, the hobos had adopted a similar system.

Jake made another decision about his quest based on this learning and observations. He would use the Purple Heart and the name Ike when dealing with potential employers or trying to get a free drink. He would use the name Hobo Jake when he was in the hobo communities. He was confident this was a good change to his plan.

Another thing Jake learned was most of the guys he met in this community were all looking for work. There were even a few women in this group. Hobos preferred the nickname of "hobo" around other hobos, as they were all seeking jobs and were willing to work for food. They actually considered themselves migrant workers, just like the Gypsies. Many were seasonal employees traveling between jobs. Interestingly, there were others traveling the rails who did not want work or jobs unless forced. They simply enjoyed the travel and did not follow the rules. Hobos called them tramps and did not want to be associated with any of their kind. They vehemently swore you couldn't trust a tramp; they would kill you and not bat an eye.

Bums were another lower-life form in the hobo hierarchy. These low lives didn't work and didn't travel; they simply stole or panhandled for support. Because of bums and tramps, hobos in general had a bad reputation in many towns.

Hobos tended to share between other hobos. At most campsites or hobo jungles, there would be a big campfire roaring with a large pot of mulligan stew containing whatever the night's residents contributed. Storytelling, information swaps and even singing were common. It seemed to Jake a similar environment to one he enjoyed with the Gypsies. Much of the storytelling was about ghosts and strange happenings. A hobo with a good story did well in the hobo jungles.

One of the rules Jake thought was extremely good was members of hobo communities would clean up the jungle every morning before continuing on their journeys. Not only did it disguise the jungle location from the cops, but the practice helped keep the landscape clean and free of litter. It also helped in with hiding in plain sight, as he had learned many years before. By now, he had developed a real love of the outdoors. He felt man was constantly spoiling the scenery with his litter and trash. He remembered the look of the battlefields before and after combat, and the slums and industrial areas in the inner city of his youth. These visual images disgusted him.

Hobos started to appear on the American scene after the Civil War. They were primarily jobless veterans and displaced farmers. Many followed the railroads west, riding for free, as they were penniless. They would sneak aboard wherever they could. The majority of the hobos were in search of jobs or land in an attempt to establish a better life. In fact, by 1906, the government estimated there were more than a half-million individuals included in the hobo category. The Great Depression of the 1930s further increased the number of hobos in the country.

Jake took to the rails on his quest to find his young Gypsy princess. At his first stop, he got the feeling that the task at hand might be a little more difficult than he had originally envisioned. Months went by, and Jake had no luck in finding her. He spent the whole first season following up on a couple of leads without the desired result. He took whatever jobs he could find; only staying long enough to get a new stake so he could begin the next step in his quest. He decided if he had no luck by the end of the first season, he would follow the carnival south and begin again in the spring.

Jake worked a variety of jobs during the off-season. Most of these were associated with being a short-order cook and dishwasher in roadside diners. He was constantly alert to any news of the Gypsies and the carnival. The biggest problem with holding a job is it kept him off the journey, postponing his quest.

Jake's second and third years were no more productive than his first. He was able to pick up a few new job skills during these years. He worked as a migrant farm worker, milking cows, picking cherries, tomatoes and apples, de-tasseling corn and even cutting grass and bailing hay. There were lots of labor-intensive jobs in the fall at harvest time. They were short-term in nature, but Jake was just looking for a stake to cover the expenses of his next step as well as current needs for food and lodging.

Jake was arrested for vagrancy, fighting and being drunk in public on an increasing frequency in the course of his journey. With each new arrest, the sentences were getting longer and longer. The cycle grew so bad that some judges began to know him by name for landing repeatedly in the same court under the same charge. An overnight stay would become three nights, and it only went up from there. The longest he had been sentenced was a ninety-day confinement.

During this time, Jake learned a few things about himself. He was losing a step or two due to his age and the aching in his joints. He was not a young man anymore. The freight trains were moving faster and bypassed many small communities, referred to by the hobo community as cannon balls. The bulls that patrolled the rail yards were getting meaner and less forgiving. Being a hobo was becoming more dangerous for an aging man. The possibility of slipping, falling, or getting run over and losing a foot or even life was an evolving fear. He did not want to be a hobo that greased the tracks, hobo language meaning someone who had been killed boarding or jumping from a moving train.

The war injury to his back further increased this problem for Jake, so he tried to confine his free rides to local milk trains. They stopped at almost every little town, carrying mail and current newspapers. They also picked up milk and cream for the local creamery or cheese plants. The travel was not fast, but he had nothing but time. Jake was starting to believe he would never find his Gypsy goddess. Yet he searched on.

During the summer of 1950, the news was all about the Koreans and the threat of a new war. Jake had had enough war and wanted no part of this new conflict. He did find that wearing the Purple Heart still got him a free drink or two almost any evening. Maybe it was fate, but one Friday evening, while wearing his medal and drinking on the house in Green Bay, Jake was arrested for public drunkenness. He was scheduled to appear before Judge Sullivan the next Monday morning.

After being returned to his cell in the municipal jail, he was allowed to talk to his two acquaintances. Mike and Dan were the names he remembered. They were around his age and had adapted to the hobo code of taking care of one another. They talked about their upcoming appearance in front of the judge. They told Jake that Judge Sullivan was good, and if you watched your p's and q's, you might catch a break and not get six months in the county lockup. If he had to, he should tell the judge he was a war hero, it wouldn't hurt. The judge was somewhat creative in his sentencing of minor offenders.

Jake was found guilty and ordered to serve a six-month sentence of hard labor at the Brown County Reforestation Camp northwest of Green Bay. Jake was not sure why he trusted these men, but only time would tell if he had made a mistake. That afternoon he was transferred with twenty-three others – Mike and Dan included – to the camp to begin their sentences.

Chapter 9

Hard Work and a Legacy

Jake had not spent much time in the city jail in Green Bay, but he knew he did not want to serve his sentence there. He knew by personal experience in his short stay that it was haunted. He had been scratched on the back and objects had been thrown at him. He had his hair pulled and was pushed across the cell. When he complained to the guards, they had no mercy for him and refused to change his cell assignment. Jake even talked to other inmates at chow about his cell. They all rolled their eyes and said it was just old Charlie up to his old, nasty behavior. Jake must have done something to upset him, as Charlie was a bitter individual and did not like people. He refused to share his home, the cell, with anyone – especially a living person.

One of the other inmates even told Jake of an inmate a year or two before who hung himself in the cell because of Charlie's abuse and harassment. They went on to say the guards didn't care because they were just a bunch of old drunks to them and deserved no better treatment.

On the ride to the camp, Jake learned his two new friends had spent the last couple of winters there on purpose, as it provided a warm place to sleep and reliable, hot food. The warden's wife did the cooking and was a good chef. There was always plenty of potatoes and fresh meat to eat, the complete opposite of living in a hobo jungle. Mike even said he had helped her on occasion, peeling potatoes and doing dishes.

The warden, a man by the name of Harry Barth, had once been a musician and played a violin with his brothers at the Riverside Ballroom in Green Bay. More recently, Barth got into cheese making, but was displaced when Straubel Cheese was bought out by Kraft and moved the operation to Chicago. He was a fair man and had a good-looking, young wife and three little girls. They lived at the camp. The wife had been a school teacher in the little town of Pine Grove, southeast of Green Bay, before marrying Harry.

Over the last couple of years with inmate labor, they had built an inmate bunkhouse and chow hall, plus living quarters for the warden and his family. There was also a shower and a couple of barns to store equipment. The inmates had been transferred every day in the morning from Green Bay to the camp, returning each evening to the county jail. They were going to be the first load of inmates to stay at the site all day and all night. Housing the inmates at the camp would be a savings for the county, and more work could be completed on a daily basis due to not having to travel forty-five minutes each way. Considering the alternatives, it wasn't too bad a deal. All a smart inmate needed to do was work hard, keep his mouth closed and his nose clean.

Jake thought this over and it all seemed fair. He also was thinking he had seen Harry play at the Riverside Ballroom several years ago. Maybe it was on his disastrous trips to Flintville, but that seemed like ages ago. He seemed to remember it was with a group called the Barth Brothers.

President Franklin D. Roosevelt's Public Works Administration was being used as a model for this camp. The voters in Brown County thought it would be better for everyone if the prisoners contributed to the county instead of sitting idly in the lockup downtown Green Bay. Judge Sullivan supported this position, deciding every man should contribute something in return for his keep. The judge had suffered the loss of a foot and did not let his disability prevent him from working. If he could do it, no prisoner should be allowed the luxury of not working – with or without a disability.

Jake figured this is why his facial scar did not get him any special consideration in sentencing, even with his Purple Heart in hand. Maybe the Heart had got him the camp option because he was a veteran.

Two weeks later, a shipment of seedling trees arrived and the planting began. It was the inmates' first major job. It seemed to Jake the hobo information network was accurate and working just fine. But if he were to continue on his quest in search of his Gypsy princess, it would have to wait until he completed his sentence.

Fire has been around since creation. Lightning and volcanic action were probably the first causes of fire on the surface of the earth and are still a source of a small percentage of today's active fires. Native man and even the native inhabitants of North America used fire in many ways beyond keeping warm and cooking food. One of these uses was clearing land for agriculture, while another centered on clearing undergrowth to improve the shooting lanes in hunting. In fact, some groups of Native Americans used fire to herd and coral animals in the wild. It was the perfect tool for this task.

As with most good things in life, there seems to be a downside that goes along with the good. Loss of control with a fire is extremely easy to do. Changing environmental conditions, lack of knowledge or just plain poor habits accounted for most of these losses. Many are preventable, but that comes with experience and learning from one's mistakes.

During the fur exploitation period by the French, use of fire increased from what the natives had practiced, due in part to more people roaming unchecked in the forests. During the logging phase of the area's history, there was a marked increase in fires. Trimmings from the fallen trees and sawdust made perfect kindling. Most of these scraps would be piled up to make access to the logs easier, but it was a giant bonfire waiting to happen, such as the Peshtigo Fire in 1871.

The city of Green Bay suffered several major fires in its history, with significant buildings destroyed in the infernos. Fire was definitely not a stranger to Northeastern Wisconsin. In fact, a 1948 fire had burned lumber and farmland around the town of Suamico. Much of the land was owned by Brown County at the time, because the farmers were suffering major crop failures from poor soil conditions and drought. Wheat farming techniques had stripped the land of nutrients, which were not being replaced quickly enough in the soil. The soil became overly dry and the winds blew it in every direction. Crop yields fell, and profits followed yields. The county had taken the land from the farmers for lack of paying their taxes.

Fire is necessary for forest regeneration. The Native Americans knew this, and had conducted selective burning on a three-year cycle to transition some forest land into agriculture. But uncontrolled, it destroys and kills without regard. The 1948 fire was a result of poor track-clearing procedures by the railroads. They would trim the growth around the track so a train could pass without hitting the branches, providing some clearance. The cuttings were piled at intervals just beyond the cleared area and left to rot. A spark from a passing locomotive provided the heat source for the fire in one of these piles. The result made the land unsellable for the county.

A plan had been developed to house and use inmate labor to reforest the valueless land in the hopes of someday putting positive money into the county treasury from the sale of the land. Jake found himself in the second phase of that plan. The facility had been built and was now moving inmates for housing. The beginning of the planting phase was about to be implemented.

Mike and Dan had been part of the first phase, which included building the facility, and were now scheduled with Jake to be included in phase two. These guys would be good resources in the future, Jake reasoned, as they had been given positions previously as "trustee-type" inmates. They had told him there were no walls, no fences and few, if any, guards around. The entire thing was more of an honor camp. At least, that is what they had told him. The truth would be evident in the future.

Because this camp was to be an open camp – a completely new concept in jails – and Mike and Dan had a couple years' experience with wardens and prison authorities, they were unofficially selected by the inmates as leaders. Good inmate leadership in a jail situation made life a bit more livable. The age and the wisdom they had would help establish camp life.

The basic hobo code of ethics was almost universally accepted. As most of these guys had been or were hobos, it became the unofficial rules in the bunkhouse. If this honor camp concept was going to work, there could not be a bunch of crazy stuff going on. Nobody was a major felon, with most of these men simply wanting to make amends for whatever minor offense they had been charged with, found guilty and sentenced. Life here involved hard work, but the living conditions were way better than anything they had experienced before. It had to be better than the haunted city jail.

Work assignments were made daily by the supervisor or warden, with men assigned by skill to the degree the supervisor felt comfortable with that individual. When the warden's wife needed help in the kitchen, Dan was usually the man assigned. When a hurt animal was found, it was usually Mike who would be put in charge of determining what and how to take care of it.

Jake saw some opportunity to let the warden know of his own mechanical and driving skills, as well as his cooking and willingness to help with the animal care. The advantages of these jobs were they required time away from the hard work of planting and the extremes of hot or cold weather. Jake's injuries also had an effect on his body. Damage to certain body parts, coupled with age, usually creates the recipe for arthritis. Jake began to feel it in his joints. He blamed the pain as the reason he was losing a step in catching a freight train in motion.

Jake was released during the winter, but was able to find his way back to the Reforestation Camp within a matter of a few days. He was pleased by this, as it didn't seem to be a bad place to spend the winter. The only problem was he was sentenced to remain there for a year, missing another summer of searching for his Gypsy princess.

Harry Barth, the camp warden, died during that next year. His wife, Aurelia Barth, was asked to continue in his place until a suitable replacement could be found. But after six months of a trial basis, she was given the job. This made her the first female supervisor in charge of a male prison facility in the country.

Jake had chatted her up one day on a trip. He had been assigned to drive her to Green Bay, and he made sure he told Mrs. Barth about his repertoire of other skills. If she ever had need for them, he would sure do a good job, he told her. It did not hurt to let the "boss" know what you could do if it gave you an advantage. Anyway, she was a good-looking woman, and her three daughters were kind of a joy to have around. Or maybe he was mellowing with his age.

Jake believed this little chat was responsible for him being assigned to help with the maintenance of the vehicles, troubleshooting and suggesting fixes when stuff broke down. He also was assigned to help Dan in the kitchen when the workload was very high. Jake even got the opportunity to help Mike with animals and build some of their cages. He felt he had not lost the old silver tongue techniques and quick mind that had helped him so greatly on the streets of Chicago. He felt alive and pleased.

Warden Harry had a dream, a plan of the camp becoming a place of beauty. It could be an outdoor textbook for children from the city, where they could learn about nature and see some of the woodland animals. He had similarly encouraged Mike to keep the animals he rescued and healed in display cages for the visiting children to see if they could not return to the wild. After his death, Aurelia continued with this side mission. Harry Barth wanted to establish an outdoors classroom for city kids to experience nature.

Aurelia thought this a great idea and fit with her teaching background. Mike liked the idea that he could spend most of his confinement caring for the animals. Harry had even pitched and convinced the county supervisor in charge of parks the value of the plan. By the time all this trickled down to Jake, he reasoned he was being offered another opportunity. All he had to do was to take advantage of it. He was feeling a part of this place. He felt he could belong. It was an odd sensation for Jake, and he wasn't sure he had ever felt this way before. Maybe this is what Jack Boyd had felt about the north woods so many years before. Jack had been gentle with his animals, the same gentleness Mike showed around the injured animals. Jake had only known animals as a source of food, but this was different and he seemed to bond with these animals. He had never had a pet.

Jake would continue serving out a sentence, be released, only to head back to the Reforestation Camp within a few weeks to serve a new sentence. This cycle went on for a couple of years. Old leaders like Dan stopped showing up every fall, and Mike was believed to have drowned in the East River one winter night after a drunken fight in Green Bay. His body had not been found in the spring when the rivers and bays tend to give up their winter kill. Therefore, Jake inherited Mike's animal duties.

Sometime around 1957, Jake failed to appear in the court system, thereby ending his Reforestation Camp life. He would have been in his early to mid-sixties at the time. Whatever happened to him is unknown, but some say his spirit lives on there.

From the first night Jake slept in bunkhouse until the last night in the 1950s, he was a storyteller. Many of his tales wove an interesting story, while others were designed to teach a point. The exception to this was when he told ghost stories, stories he said he heard from his Gypsy princess back in his carnival days. He claimed to have spent many long days and nights discussing ghosts and the supernatural with her. He confessed he did not believe at first and was only faking interest to be close to the young woman. But in time, he started to believe their existence.

He spoke of some limited first-hand experiences and had collected many good stories over the years, only because he had listened and tried to learn. Jake even reported to the other inmates that he was confident the camp was haunted and he had seen things at night he could not explain. He believed it was the first warden, Harry Barth, Aurelia Barth's husband and father of the three little girls that lived at the camp. This usually hushed the room and he would slip into a story. Most were not lengthy, as the guys worked hard all day and fell asleep quickly out of sheer exhaustion. Jake thought this also helped protect the young girls by telling the guys that the girls had a ghost protecting them. He knew how to weave a convincing tale.

Jake said the area near the camp was a prime area for haunting. He mentioned the sacred native burial grounds and the fact they had been disturbed by the white settlers. He had a story about John Jacob Astor destroying one of these sites so he could get a street installed where he wanted it. At the time, Astor was trying to build the village of Astor, which later would become part of the new city of Green Bay. Jake said Astor was seen throwing the grave markers into the Fox River. Jake said that for years after, the natives roamed the adjacent area, looking for revenge.

Jake told stories of the grisly murder downtown in the YMCA and how the third floor of that building has been haunted ever since. He had stories of a young woman still waiting at the train depot in downtown Green Bay for the return of her beau from the First World War, where he had been killed. The woman could not acknowledge the fact, hanging herself in the depot.

He also had stories about gruesome murders of the working girls at the brothels in Howard and on old Willow Street in Green Bay. Jake said noises could still be heard on dark nights of the girls imprisoned in the basements of one of these brothels. The bones of one had been found buried near the furnace. There was even a story about the woman who owned and worked the Union Hotel in De Pere, just south of Green Bay. She was seen many times taking inventory of goods, and checking the work of the cooks and bartender to make sure her customers were getting what they paid for. She was also seen going into the room that had been hers on the second floor. When followed, she vanished.

Jake maintained that ghosts were everywhere. He said he preferred to be at the camp, as the ghost at the downtown jail was not a friendly ghost. The one here seemed to be friendly, at least for now.

Jake told of his Gypsy princess going to the chapel near Champion, northeast of Green Bay, where in 1859 a school girl named Adele Brise had seen multiple visions of the Blessed Mother. The girl had been instructed to educate children in the faith, and she would go on to found a school and an order of nuns. The chapel built on the site was the only spot spared from the Peshtigo Fire after it jumped to the east side of the bay. The flames charred only the outside of the wooden fence posts around the edge of the property, sparing the chapel, school and convent.

Jake made clear this last story might be nothing but religious mumbo jumbo, but the princess and other faithful truly believed it. If a vision with a message was not a ghost, then he didn't know what was. The princess had always said she talked to ghosts and that ghosts had a message for us. All we had to do was listen and learn.

Listeners always asked Jake if ghosts should be feared, because as children they had been warned to be good or the "boogey man" would get them. They also feared ghosts living under their beds. What did the princess have to say about that?

Jake would respond that he, too, had thought most of the talk about ghosts was nothing but kid stuff. But to his surprise, the princess truly believed and talked to the dead. She never once referred to her customers as "marks," which many of the carnies did. This fact alone, Jake said, was almost enough for him to change his mind and believe. It was only after seeing Harry Barth checking on the bunkhouse and the sleeping inmates late at night with his own eyes that he was completely persuaded.

When pressed for more information, Jake would respond he was with Harry the day he died. Jake was the driver on a trip back from Green Bay when Harry had a heart attack. He was near death as they approached the camp. Sensing death was near, Harry made Jake swear an oath to protect Harry's family and assure their safety at the camp. Additionally, Jake was to do whatever he could to assure his vision of an educational opportunity for local children became a reality.

As a result of this oath, Harry would come back to check on Jake and his progress from time to time. Jake would then say, "I won't let the man down! I swore an oath to him as he died. I've got to fulfill that oath."

Epilogue

Jake was not a formally educated man, but a man of many experiences. He claimed there are many types of ghosts, the bulk of them good versus the evil ones many fear. Further, these good ghosts fall into a few major categories. Three of these are: ghosts with unfinished business; ghosts with materialistic attachments; and ghosts that are messengers. Jake fits all three of these categories.

Possibilities regarding Jake's failure to return to the camp with the onset of cold weather are numerous. It could have been the result of an accident, or he may have ended up greasing the rails on his continued quest. This would also give him unfinished business at the NEW Zoo to fulfill his oath. Harry, as well, had unfinished business at the zoo to see his vision come to reality. Aurelia Barth passed away a few years before the completion of the final two building projects at the camp. She, too, could have unfinished business at the zoo.

It is easy to see a material attachment to the area for Jake, as it was the only place he truly loved and felt a connection. Harry's wife, Aurelia, could have easily be the replacement for Jake's feeling of love for his grandma, for Daisy, or even for his Gypsy princess, each equally containing notes of unfinished business.

In fact, two of the most recent ghostly encounters have been in these two newest buildings. Both of these encounters were inspections late at night with doors opened and lights checked, as if to receive a final approval. The most recent occurred after midnight, when a zookeeper was cleaning the new education building. He was confronted by an unseen person asking what he was doing. He turned to answer, yet saw no one. Could this have been Jake?

The current speculation is Harry and Aurelia are reunited and Jake continues to wander, attempting to accomplish the vision Harry set for the zoo and camp so many years ago. It is a vision that might never be completely finished. What is the takeaway from all this? If you have an encounter with a ghost at the Reforestation Camp and NEW Zoo, it is probably old Hobo Jake doing his rounds in fulfillment of his sworn duty.

My friend Louie would conclude the story with a definitive statement that the proceeding was the truth, the whole truth, nothing but the truth. He had heard it directly from the horse's mouth: Jake's ghost. Finally, and with a glint in his eye, Louie would say, "And if you don't believe me now, well, you're just a dumb turd."

Acknowledgements

Thanks go out to many who provided inspiration and background information, including:

Carl Behrend, for his novel, "The Legend of the Christmas Ship"; Pam Sievert, for her book, "Into the Woods: The Story of Aurelia Barth and the Reforestation Camp"; Jack Rudolph, for his articles in the *Green Bay Press-Gazette*; "The Green Bay Area History and Legend"; Castle Publications, for its book, "Tales of the Great Lakes"; Todd Clements, for his work on the "Haunts of Mackinac"; and to many of my friends and acquaintances for stories, ideas, information and encouragement.

Special thanks go out to Ruth Boettcher for helping get me in contact with the editorial and publishing team at M&B Global Solutions Inc.: Bonnie Groessl, Mike Dauplaise and Amy Mrotek. I would never have gotten my story to print without their knowledge, skill, guidance and help.

I would also like to thank my fishing buddy, Louie Black. I hope you enjoyed the read.

About the Author

Jim Turner is a retired engineer who volunteers at the NEW Zoo several times per month. This is his first work of fiction.

Jim relocated to the Green Bay, Wisconsin, area for employment reasons and has learned to love the area he now calls home. There is much history to the region beyond the Green Bay Packers and beauty that is underreported. His goal is to share his appreciation of the region with readers everywhere.